"My brakes aren't working, Seb. And Timmy's with me!"

Tacy's voice was tight with fear over the phone.

"Did you try shifting down to low gear?" Seb asked.

"It didn't work. And I pulled the emergency brake, but it only engaged for a second."

"Okay. In a half mile, you'll come to a fork in the road. Go left, and the pavement will level out. That might reduce your speed. When the car stops moving, try to force it into Park. I'll be right behind you."

"Left," she repeated.

Please let this work, Seb thought. There was no way this was just an occurrence of faulty brakes.

Tacy's voice cracked on the console. "Seb, there's a truck in front of me that's barely moving. I'm heading off the road..." Her voice faded.

Tacy's car bumped off the tarmac and dived into the gully, thumping straight down into a field stretching into the horizon as far as the eye could see...

Jaycee Bullard hails from Minnesota, where a thirty-degree day in January is reason to break out short-sleeved shirts. In the ten years since graduating with a degree in classical languages, Jaycee has worked as a paralegal, an office manager and a Montessori teacher. An earlier version of *Framed for Christmas* won the 2016 ACFW Genesis award for Romantic Suspense. Check in and say hi on Facebook at Facebook.com/jaycee.bullard.1.

Books by Jaycee Bullard

Love Inspired Suspense

Framed for Christmas
Fatal Ranch Reunion

FATAL RANCH REUNION

JAYCEE BULLARD

LOVE INSPIRED SUSPENSE

INSPIRATIONAL ROMANCE

LOVE INSPIRED SUSPENSE
INSPIRATIONAL ROMANCE

Recycling programs
for this product may
not exist in your area.

ISBN-13: 978-1-335-72188-4

Fatal Ranch Reunion

Copyright © 2020 by Jean Bullard

This edition published by arrangement with Harlequin Books S.A.

For questions and comments about the quality of this book, please contact us
at CustomerService@Harlequin.com.

Love Inspired
22 Adelaide St. West, 40th Floor
Toronto, Ontario M5H 4E3, Canada
www.Harlequin.com

Printed in U.S.A.

For there is nothing covered, that shall not be revealed;
neither hid, that shall not be known.
—Luke 12:2

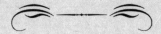

To the new littles—Benny, Hannah, Charlotte, Johnny and Ollie—sorry you were missed the first time around!

And with boundless appreciation to JGB for your tireless support and patience in reading and rereading my stories. And a special thanks for your colorful depiction of a black widow spider.

ONE

Tacy Tolbert clutched the handlebars of the ATV and swept her eyes across the once familiar landscape of her grandfather's North Dakota ranch. If the sale went through as expected, some other family would soon own all of this land. The rolling hills. The rocky cliffs. Everything but the dusty trail that marked the border between the Tolberts' property and the Hunts'. The trail was disputed territory. Never-neverland, they used to call it back in the day.

Back in the day. Ten years ago. It felt like a lifetime.

As she leaned into a turn, a strange sort of exhaustion pressed against her brain, and her mind drifted back to all those summers before she turned eighteen. It felt like a cliché to call those days golden, but back then, it sure had seemed like something quite wonderful was there for the taking. Steven. Seb. She closed her eyes and conjured their faces and imagined a life that might have been.

A bump shook the chassis of the ATV. Her eyes blinked open, and her head jerked up. Instinct guided her fingers to the kill switch under the right handlebar. With a shudder and a cough, the vehicle lurched to a hard stop, jolting her body forward, nearly knocking her to the ground.

What? Where? One minute she was sightseeing along the trail, and the next, she was stalled in the middle of a pasture. Her hands shook as reality dawned. She had fallen asleep at the wheel of the ATV.

She swiped a damp palm across her eyes. She needed to move around, to shake off the fog of bewilderment blanketing her brain. She slid down from the seat and forced herself to walk, but her muscles felt like jelly, unable to maintain an upright stance. Why was she so tired? She had logged ten hours of sleep last night in the guest room at the ranch. But somehow, without warning, weariness had crept into her bones, pulling at her eyelids, dulling her thoughts. She looked down at the carpet of withered grass at her feet. Would anyone care if she lay down and took a little nap? All she needed was a couple of minutes to take the edge off, just long enough to keep herself from nodding off again on the ride back home.

She pressed her face to the ground. That felt good. So good. She stretched out her legs and curled up on her side. The scent of the cool dirt took her back to days of swimming at the water hole, eating fried chicken, and then napping in the shade of the old elm tree. Timmy would love this. Almost ten, he was just old enough to explore on his own and young enough to still revel in the adventure. But it was too late for that. Even if her grandfather changed his mind about selling, she could never bring Timmy here.

Never. This place held too many secrets. Secrets she planned to keep from her son.

Bam! A blast of gunfire split the air, followed by the thud of hooves in the distance. She pushed up on her elbows and looked across a meadow dappled with yarrow and coneflowers. And then she saw it.

A lone buffalo stood on the crest of the hill, its two long horns curving outward from its head. She rubbed her eyes as six more bison positioned themselves alongside him, shaggy in their light summer coats, their unruly tufts of fur flapping in the wind. Behind them, the rest of the Hunts' herd lined up, ready to stampede.

She needed to move. And fast. Her heartbeat pounded in her ears. *Go, go.* But which way?

Should she sprint back to the ATV or head for the trees?

The trees. She stood up and took a woozy step toward the pines. She staggered. Wobbled. Tumbled to the ground. There was something horrifyingly familiar about this dizziness and exhaustion, the tired muscles, the overwhelming malaise. It brought back a memory of waking in the hospital after the accident. But how was it possible that she was experiencing those same drugged sensations today? She struggled to stand as her legs once again collapsed from under her and her arms flailed ineffectively to break her fall.

If she couldn't run, she could crawl. She pushed herself forward, hand over hand, toward the edge of the field. A tall tree in the middle of the stand became her beacon. She'd climb that pine and hide in the branches until the herd passed her by.

Beneath her palms, the ground trembled. The buffalo were on the move. Her fingers scraped through the grass and the dirt. *Faster, faster.* She raised her eyes to the sight of dozens of bison streaming over the hill.

Her stomach lurched as the hopelessness of her predicament became clear. She was less than ten feet from the trees, but she wasn't going to make it. She was going to be trampled in the stampede.

"Help!" Desperation knotted in her throat. She couldn't die like this, groggy and confused in the middle of a field. But the buffalo were close and getting closer, grunting and groaning. Fear exploded in her chest. This was it. There was no way to escape. Her arms trembled as a two-thousand-pound behemoth charged toward her, his long, curved horns capable of tearing her limbs apart.

No, No. Please, God. Help me.

"Go away!" she screamed. "Leave me alone." Marshaling her last reserves of strength, she pulled herself upright and flapped her arms. "Get out of here. Now."

A mechanical growl cut through the din. Beams of sunlight bounced off the chrome frame of a red motorcycle rocketing along the trail. Leaning in tight against the handlebars, the rider revved the motor, cutting ahead of the herd as he circled to the spot where she was standing.

"Don't move," the voice from behind the reflective helmet said.

As if I could.

She froze in place as the rider spun around and raced up the hill.

The buffalo veered to the left to get out of

the way, snorting as the bike rumbled a thunderous retort. Again and again, the rider drove against the herd, nudging the outliers closer to the rest, until the last of the bison relocated to the far end of the pasture.

I'm safe. She sank to her knees as relief washed over her senses. Relief *and* gratitude toward the stranger who had saved her life. *Stranger?* Her breath caught in her throat. Ten years was a long time, but back then, only one boy she knew owned a red motorcycle. Steven Hunt. He had been her friend until the accident reignited a century-old feud, drove a wedge between their families, and forced her and her father to move away.

The motorcycle pulled back up beside her.

"Steven?" The words were on her lips before she realized her mistake. The rider had the same slim build as Steven. The same broad shoulders. The same confident air. But even before he bent his head and pulled off his helmet, she knew.

Her rescuer wasn't Steven Hunt. He was Seb, Steven's twin brother. The boy she had married when she was eighteen. The man who had left her at her darkness moment. The father of a child he didn't know had been born.

Seb Hunt swung his right leg over the seat of the motorcycle and rushed toward Tacy. Almost a decade serving as an MP on military bases across the globe had taught him to expect the unexpected, but the sight of his ex-wife kneeling in the grass, her face a mask of confusion and pain, shook him to his core.

Adrenaline fueled the questions clamoring in his brain. How had the bison escaped from the enclosure? Had someone forgotten to close the gate? Why was Tacy here, in the middle of the pasture? And why hadn't she taken off running when the first of the herd crested the hill?

He took a deep breath to calm his jangled nerves and knelt down beside her. "Are you okay?"

She stared up at him, her eyes glazed with shock. Was she as stunned to see him as he was to see her? He shook his head, reminding himself that it wasn't important now. Whatever her reasons, she was here—and she'd almost died. He needed to know she was all right…but she seemed so shaken that he wasn't even sure she could hear his voice or understand what he was asking her. He tried again. "Tacy. Why are you here?"

She tugged at the sleeve of her white cotton shirt and stared at the ground. "I came to see my grandfather. He's married now, and he's decided to sell the ranch."

"I heard about that." Carl Tolbert's decision to

pack up and leave Chimney Bluff was all folks seemed to talk about these days. "We can catch up on that later. But can you try to tell me what happened here today?"

She fixed him with a blurry stare. "I've been thinking a lot about my dad since he passed, so I took the ATV for a drive to look at the ranch. I stopped to take a rest. And then…" She shook her head as if she was trying to clear her brain. "I must have fallen asleep because a gunshot woke me up. And the whole herd came charging over the hill."

What? Keith Tolbert was dead? Odd, that with all of his family's talk about the Tolberts, no one had thought to mention that fact.

"Wow, Tace. I'm sorry to hear about your father."

"I miss him a lot."

"I bet you do." Keith Tolbert had lived his life for his only daughter. And Tacy had been on the path of achieving something great. Until… His breath caught in his throat. The details of that last summer burned through his memory like a hot coal. But he couldn't let his mind go back to that place. Ten years had passed. And for reasons Seb had yet to ascertain, Tacy had come home.

"When you saw the bison, why didn't you head for the trees?"

Her eyes blinked in and out of focus as she tried to hold his gaze. "I tried. But I was having trouble moving my legs."

He pulled out his phone. "We need to get you to the doctor's and have you checked out."

"I… I think I'm okay," Tacy said, pushing herself up. A trickle of blood trailed down her arm and pooled in the dirt. "I'm just…really out of it for some reason. I'd chalk it up to adrenaline, but it started before the stampede." She shook her head. "I don't know what's wrong."

"If nothing else, that gash on your arm looks pretty deep. It may need stitches. And the grass is covered with buffalo droppings. Have you had a tetanus shot in the last five years?"

"I don't think so."

"Okay. You'll probably want to get that taken care of right away. In the meantime, I'll call one of your ranch hands to pick you up." He punched seven digits into his phone. Hard to believe that after all these years, he still remembered the direct line to the Tolberts'.

"Hello," a low voice grumbled into the phone.

"Hey, this is Seb Hunt. I'm out on the east pasture with Tacy Tolbert, and she's pretty shook up. Someone may have left the buffalo gate open on our property, and she was almost trampled by the herd… Right, right, I'll see you soon."

He clicked off the phone and looked at Tacy. She still didn't seem completely aware or alert. If this was adrenaline, it should have started to level out by now. He was starting to get concerned that something was seriously wrong.

"Do you have any idea what's making you so groggy?"

"No. I slept well last night, and I felt well rested when I first woke up this morning."

"Could it be low sugar? Did you have anything to eat or drink for breakfast?"

Her eyes flickered. "A muffin and an apple. And my grandfather's new wife, Lois, made me a cup of coffee before I left."

"Okay." It was a huge leap to assume that some sort of drug had been slipped into Tacy's beverage. But how else to explain her reckless decision to nap in the middle of a field? Even after ten years in the city, she ought to have remembered how dangerous it was to lie down in a pasture where horses and cattle grazed nearby and trucks cut an easy path across the open land.

Of course, there was always the simplest explanation—that she might have voluntarily taken something to help her sleep and the residual effects were still in her system. It seemed unlikely, but anything was possible, especially if Tacy was still grieving the loss of her dad. And those pills could really mess with your head. He'd seen his fair share of senseless stunts from soldiers under the influence of sleep aids.

"Did you…take anything else? Maybe something last night to calm you down?"

He could see the dawning light of comprehension—and indignation—in her eyes. "You think I'm on drugs?"

"No. I'm just trying to make sense of this whole situation." A shiver shot up his spine as he considered what might have happened if he hadn't been able to redirect the herd. Tacy might have died.

He couldn't even think about that. He needed to figure out what was going on. It was hard to believe, but maybe living in Denver had dulled Tacy's once-sharp cowgirl senses. Maybe she was embarrassed to admit she'd been using sleeping pills, believing he'd judge her for it. Or maybe she had too many things on her mind, like a job or a new relationship. A sharp pang of jealousy tugged at his heart. Even after all this time, it was hard to accept that she had moved on without him. He blew a long breath through his nose, searching for something to say that wouldn't upset her or reopen old wounds. "So, did you end up going to law school and fulfilling your lifelong dream?"

Tacy blinked. "Who said that was my dream?"

Her father, that was who. But this wasn't the moment for a deep dive into the past, especially since Keith Tolbert was no longer around to present his side of the story.

"Sorry. I just thought…"

"No. I'm sorry—I didn't mean to snap. I did go to law school, so there must be some truth to what you said after all."

Tires crunched against the ground as a tan F-150 negotiated the bend on the path toward the pasture. Len Jones pulled to a stop and hopped out of the cab. Despite his age, he was still tall and gangly, the kind of cowboy that used to be featured in the old Westerns Seb and his brother had watched when they were kids.

Len's face brightened as it lit upon Tacy.

"Hi, there, Tacy. You're a sight for sore eyes. Your grandfather's sure glad to have you back for a visit. Hey, there Seb. Good to see you, too. On my way out here, I drove by the enclosure and checked out the gate. Just like you said, it was wide open. I don't get how it happened. Last night when I passed by the border while doing my rounds, everything looked locked up nice and tight."

"Did you see anyone this morning in the vicinity of the pen?" Seb asked.

Len ran a wrinkled hand across the stubble on his chin. "Just your brother. He was there around dawn, checking out the stock and tossing a stick for that new puppy of yours. But I can't believe he'd leave the gate open. He'd never make that kind of mistake."

"Well, somebody did." Seb clamped his lips shut and resisted saying more. He'd check the gate out himself and then talk to Steve when he got home.

Tacy turned and walked toward the truck. She climbed into the passenger seat and pulled the door closed. Should he offer to drive her to see a doctor? It didn't seem likely that she would take him up on it, but it was worth a shot. He poked his head through the open window. "I have to take Steven's bike home, but how about I pick you up in a half hour and take you to the clinic?"

Something changed in her countenance, and her eyes clouded with wariness. "That won't be necessary. I can ask my grandfather for a ride."

Her grandfather. Right. Of course, she'd chosen a Tolbert over a Hunt. So that was it, then. Except for the one last question tugging at his brain. "You said something about hearing a gunshot right before the stampede?"

Her forehead wrinkled. "I did?"

"Yeah. Could you tell where it came from?"

She fixed her glance on him, and his heart somersaulted in his chest. He had forgotten that her brown eyes always gave away whatever emotion she was feeling. Joy. Sadness. Anxiety.

Right now, they were dark and guarded. "Why does it matter?"

He didn't have a good answer, just a gut feeling that there were too many odd factors at play to chalk up to coincidence. "I'm not sure it does, but I'm going to check the perimeter of the pen to look for shells and maybe figure out where the shooter was standing. In the meantime, you should ask for a drug screen at the clinic. Just in case you accidentally ingested something that could be making you groggy."

Tacy nodded. He half-expected her to ask how he thought she might have "accidentally ingested" something strong enough to cause her to fall asleep at the wheel of the ATV. When she didn't, he was glad. For the moment, he'd keep his concerns under wraps, at least until he had the chance to inspect the area around the gate. He stepped away from the truck as Len revved the engine and cranked the wheel.

He waited for the dust to settle before heading on foot across the pasture. Before him, the field stretched like a dappled carpet under a canopy of blue, the variegated grasses giving way to the purple and yellow wildflowers along the edge of the hill.

But he couldn't allow the beauty of the land to

distract him from his mission. He wanted to see the open gate and empty enclosure for himself and draw his own conclusions. It all came down to the question of whether someone had deliberately tried to harm Tacy. And if so, why? But on that particular subject, he wasn't sure where to start. He didn't know anything about her life in Colorado. After she left Chimney Bluff, she had ignored all of his attempts to reach out and discuss what had happened between them. He had sent dozens of letters and made hundreds of calls, but she had never replied. Until she sent him the paperwork for the divorce.

Enough. His MP training had taught him to compartmentalize his feelings, to concentrate his focus on the task before him. When he reached the top of the hill, he trained his glance on the bison enclosure. Sure enough, the gate was open. He studied the ground, but the grass was too dry to reveal footprints. He walked a few paces. It didn't add up. Could Tacy be wrong about the gunshot? She said that the blast woke her up. But maybe it was some other sound that she mistook for the crack of a gun firing.

Still, he wanted to talk to his brother. If Steven had left the gate open, that was just plain carelessness. Someone needed to remind him that he was almost thirty now, not some immature teenager obsessed with riding bulls. Seb clenched his jaw. The fact that Steven could be so reckless made his blood boil. Because of his mistake, Tacy had almost been killed.

He turned and began to walk toward the spot where he had left the motorcycle. As he passed by the gate, his eye caught the glint of metal on the ground. He bent down and reached for it, his fingers rummaging in the dirt before locking on a small cylinder. A rifle shell, fresh and shiny. And recently fired, if he could believe the telltale gunpowder tang still clinging to the metal.

Once again, instinct kicked in, causing him to consider the possibility that the open gate had been something more than a careless mistake. And maybe—just maybe—his gut was right, and Tacy was the intended target of a near-deadly attack.

TWO

Tacy's visit to the clinic had gone just as she had expected. The doctor had stitched the gash on her arm and administered the injection with speedy precision.

Better safe than sorry, her father used to say. But did getting a tetanus shot ensure that she was safe? Seb had asked a lot of questions about her state of mind leading up to the accident. And he had seemed awfully interested in the gunshot she had heard right before the stampede. But why would anyone want to hurt her? This was Chimney Bluff. The only people who even knew that she was home were her grandfather and Lois and a handful of workers at the ranch. If only her father was here to help her understand what was going on.

Oh, Dad. I miss you so much.

She took a deep breath. She felt so much better now that she had gotten checked out at the clinic. And while she was there, she'd asked for—and received—a drug test as Seb had recommended. The results would take a while to process, but the doctor had tried to ease her concerns by pointing out that the fatigue she had experienced earlier might be just a normal reaction to months of exhaustion and stress. It was a plausible diagnosis, especially after she explained that she'd had hardly a minute to relax between finishing her course work, studying for the bar exam, and caring for her dad. Add guilt and sadness to the mix, and there were no margins left to keep things in perspective.

No wonder she kept fixating on the strange coincidence that Seb had been the one to ride to her rescue. A blush of heat rose in her cheeks at the memory. When he took off his helmet and she saw his face, a familiar jolt of attraction had surged through her veins. She had forgotten how she used to feel when they were together. But those emotions needed to remain tucked away in the deepest part of her heart.

She paused in the shade of the building to allow her eyes to adjust to the white-hot glare of the afternoon sun. Typical late summer in western North Dakota. Hot and dry.

"Tacy!"

She looked across the parking lot and saw Seb heading toward her. He placed a dusty boot on the curb where she was standing. "Everything okay?"

"I got the shot." She twisted her arm to show him to bandage. "And they took a swab of my saliva to do a drug screen as well."

"How long before you get the results?"

"The nurse said it might take a couple of days. What are you doing here?"

"Looking for you. I called the ranch, and Len told me that you had gone to the clinic. I wanted to fill you in on what I found when I checked the buffalo enclosure. The latch on the gate was intact—someone opened it on purpose. And I found a spent shell in the grass about ten feet away. The powder residue smelled fresh, so I assume it came from a rifle that was recently fired."

Tacy's heart sank. She'd hoped she'd been wrong about that. "I was pretty out of it when I woke up, but it's good to know that I didn't imagine the gunshot." A shiver of fear ran up her spine as she recalled the sight of the buffalo approaching. What if she had died right there? Who would raise Timmy?

At the thought of her son—enrolled at a camp in eastern Wyoming, less than a hundred miles away—a knot of anxiety coiled in her gut. Seb was Timmy's dad. If she had been killed in the stampede, would he have stepped in to care for their son?

She hoped so. But she couldn't be sure.

"Tacy?" Seb raised a brow. "You okay?"

"I'm good. I was just thinking about what might have happened if you hadn't come along when you did."

"Yeah, well. It all worked out, didn't it?" His dark eyes crinkled as he smiled, and her heart jumped in her chest. It was almost as if…

Stop it, she told herself. *He abandoned you, remember? Left you crushed and heartbroken, and then he filed for divorce.* She wouldn't let herself go all moony-eyed and soft. She pushed back her shoulders and stood a little straighter.

"Right," she said as she turned away from him. "I better go. Thanks again."

She barely heard his hesitant goodbye. She fumbled through her purse for her sunglasses, slipped them on and swiveled around just in time to see Seb climb into a green truck parked only a few spaces away from her Nissan.

"Bye, Seb," she said as she reached for the handle of her vehicle.

Even though the sunroof was open, her car felt like an oven when she climbed inside. She flipped on the air conditioner and opened the windows. As soon as the temperature cooled down, she'd close everything up and be on her way. But as she reached behind her to click on her seat belt, an unsettled feeling pulsed across her chest. She craned her neck to check the empty back seat and then looked up through the sunroof at the branches of the tree overhanging the space. She shifted her right foot onto the gas petal, and something brushed against her leg.

A scream stuck in her throat as a rattlesnake slithered out from under the seat and raised its head to stare back at her, its dark, beady eyes calculating and alert.

She blew out a long, silent breath. She needed to stay calm and ignore the fact that a thick, scaly tail was loosely coiled inches from her ankle.

Memories from ten years ago cascaded through her brain. Hadn't she survived for five hours trapped on a narrow ledge three hundred feet above the ground? That day on the cliff, there had been snakes among the rocks. But she hadn't flinched or panicked back then. She had stayed strong.

It was time to summon that same courage again.

A desperate scheme took shape in her head. If she could get her legs off the floor, she could push herself through the sunroof and out of the snake's range. Lifting herself through the opening would be difficult, but not impossible.

She leaned back against her seat and lifted her right leg one inch at a time until her foot was level with the seat. Her heart jackhammered as the rattler's tongue slipped in and out of its mouth, teasing and threatening. She closed her eyes and prayed for fortitude. *Help me, God. You were there for me on the rocky ledge. You gave me strength that I never knew I possessed. And You created me to be smarter than any old snake.*

Now the easy part. She raised her right arm and looped her fingers around the rim of the sunroof. Once she secured her grip, she did the same on the opposite side with her left hand. Now all she needed to do was lift her left leg onto the seat and boost herself through the roof without triggering the snake to strike.

A movement on her left caught her attention. Seb was out of his vehicle, his eyes dark and questioning.

"Rattlesnake," she mouthed.

He shook his head.

"Rattlesnake," she repeated, desperate to make him understand.

A second later, his face appeared at the window. His eyes flickered to the snake knotted on the floor.

"Okay. I see it," he said.

She shifted her body against the back of her

seat to make space for her other leg. Terror seeped down her spine as the rattler's triangular head pulsated on its neck, charting her every move. *Don't look at it.* She forced herself to stare straight ahead as her foot dangled inches from the floor. *Don't look.* Her muscles began to quiver. Out of the corner of her eye, she could see the snake's forked tongue stab the air and hear its tail's deadly rattle.

Don't look.

But she couldn't resist one quick glance at those flickering eyes and that yawning open mouth that seemed ready to…*snap.*

The rattler struck.

Seb wrenched open the handle, yanked Tacy from the driver's seat, and slammed the door behind them. She went limp in his arms as he carried her to the curb and set her down.

"Stay calm. I'll get help." He pulled his cell from his pocked, punching in two numbers before she stopped him with a touch of her hand.

"I'm okay. Its fangs didn't penetrate my boot."

He let out a long breath. Maybe the rattler hadn't shot its venom into her system, but the close call must have set her heart racing.

His heart was racing. He needed to get a grip on his feelings and stay focused.

"You can wait in my truck while I call someone to get the snake out of your car."

He offered her his arm and she accepted it as she pulled herself up, but then she released it immediately. He opened the door and waited until she was settled in the passenger seat. Then he walked around to the rear of the vehicle and placed a call to the sheriff. By the time he climbed into the driver's seat, his shirt was damp with perspiration. He inserted his key in the ignition, and the whir of the air conditioner pulsed through the vents.

"It should cool off in a few minutes." He glanced at Tacy, who was sitting ramrod straight, her eyes fixed ahead. "You sure you're okay?"

"I'm fine," she said.

She didn't look fine. Her face was pale, and her arms were trembling. "The dispatcher said they'd have a truck here in the next half hour. So, all we have to do is wait."

"Thank you again for coming to my rescue."

"From where I was standing, you were doing a good job of handling that rattler yourself. I can't believe how calm you were."

"Calm? I didn't feel calm. I felt desperate."

"Yeah, well, that was an extremely scary situation. Like what happened this morning with the buffalo. Has it occurred to you that the two incidents might be connected?"

Tacy's lips pursed. "It's not that strange, is it? I left the sunroof open and parked under a tree."

"Rattlesnakes don't climb trees."

"Sometimes they do."

She folded her arms, and nostalgia panged in his chest. For a moment it felt like they were ten years old and arguing about whose horse won the race across the pasture.

"Okay. Fine," he conceded. "Maybe it's possible for a snake to fall out of a tree and through an open sunroof into a car parked underneath. But isn't it also possible that something more serious is going on? In the last six hours, you've already had two near-death experiences."

Tacy shook her head. "I understand what you are saying, Seb. But it's a huge leap to assume that someone is trying to kill me."

"But what about the shell I found in the grass?"

"You know as well as I do that it could have been on the ground for weeks."

Hadn't he told her that the powder smelled fresh? But she clearly didn't want to hear it. "All I'm saying is that you need to be careful. Because in all the time I've spent on the ranch, no one has ever left the gate to the buffalo enclosure open. No one. Ever. And I have never heard of a rattler falling from a tree." He reached over and picked up the notes he had scribbled on the back of an envelope. "While you were inside the clinic, I did an online search to see what I could find out about your grandfather's new wife. It took a bit of digging, but I all I discovered was that her maiden name was Cloverfield and that she used to live in Reno."

Tacy's eyes widened. "Why did you do that? What does Lois have to do with any if this?"

"I haven't figured out that part out yet. But think about it, Tace. A long-lost granddaughter arrives in town and threatens the status quo. It's pretty weak as a motive, but if the tox screen comes back positive for a sedative, it might be something worth considering."

A shadow of anxiety passed over her face. "Look, Seb. I should have mentioned this earlier, but I'm headed home tomorrow. This was only a short visit to give my grandfather a letter from my dad."

What? Seb turned his head to hide his dismay. Tacy only planned to stay in Chimney Bluff for one more day? He had been hoping that at some point they could have a real conversation. Not that he expected them to look into each other's eyes and decide that the divorce was a mistake. No. That was water under the bridge, as his mom liked to say. But this could be his only chance to talk.

"I'm surprised your grandfather didn't convince you to stay longer."

Tacy hesitated. "I actually haven't told him that I'm leaving yet. He's not going to like it, but I need to get home. I have a lot going on."

Life seemed to be pulling her in a couple of different directions. He got it. He had options, too. Six weeks ago, when he resigned his military commission, working the land and running the ranch had seemed like an ideal respite from the uncertainty of life in war-torn countries across the globe. But an unexpected job offer with the FBI in Washington, DC had given him pause. The agency had allowed him ample time to make a decision, but, at this point, the six-week grace period had dwindled down to two.

He looked at his watch. "The snake removal guy should be here shortly."

"Chimney Bluff has a snake removal guy?"

"They'll probably send the lowest ranking deputy from the station."

Sure enough, when the blue-and-white squad car pulled into the lot, the officer in charge looked like a kid excited about his first real case as he began to unload his equipment from the trunk.

"So," Seb said after a minute passed in silence. "You like being a lawyer?"

Tacy shot him a look. "I don't know yet. I just took the bar exam, so I have to wait and see if I passed."

"You'll pass." No doubt about it. Tacy had been top of her class in high school with a bright future ahead. Until he had messed everything up with his crazy idea that they should get married and run away. "You've always been smart as a whip," he continued.

"Maybe I wasn't so smart, all things considered."

Wow. Her zinger hit its mark. He looked away, fighting to gain control. Was she insinuating that marrying him had been a bad decision? Even though it was true, the implication hurt. And it served the intended purpose and shut him up.

"I guess I should be taking off, then," Tacy said. "Thanks again for everything, Seb. Maybe next time I'm in town we can catch up."

Tacy reached for the handle of the truck's door. In one more second, she'd be gone.

"Wait," he said. "Do you have five more minutes to talk?"

Tacy swiveled around to face him. "What do you want to talk about?"

What didn't he want to talk about? The accident. The radio silence. The divorce. Most of all, he wanted to know why something that started with so much promise had ended in such a horrible way. The woman he married was strong and kind and always forgiving. So why had she shut him out and run away?

But where to begin? He might as well start with the accident on Shepherd's Peak. The guilt still remained when he thought about that moment when Tacy lost her footing and began to fall. The sight of her body bouncing backwards against the rocks and crumpling onto the ledge was part one of a horror reel of the worst moments of his life.

"I was hoping we could discuss what happened on the cliff," he said. "I'd like to hear what you remember."

Tacy quirked her lips into a sad smile. "Really?"

He nodded, so she continued. "Well, I recall that it was a sunny day. We were still excited about being married, even though it had only been ten days. I can't remember which one of us came up with the idea of scaling the peak, but I know that we both thought it would be a good place to say goodbye to the land before we left for Texas."

He winced. It had been his idea, along with the plan to take Tacy back to Fort Hood. A bold move, particularly given the bad blood between their families. But they were in love. What could go wrong?

Tacy's wistful smile faded as she continued. "I remember that the climb was challenging, but I was keeping up. I definitely recall feeling that I had the skills to make it to the top. But then, I lost my grip and started to fall. After that?" She shrugged. "You were screaming my name, and I couldn't do anything to stop myself from hitting the rocks. When I landed on the ledge, you came up beside me and said you were going to get help and that you'd be right back. Funny. I was thinking about that today when I saw the rattler—how there were snakes all around me up there and how I tried so hard to be brave. Anyway. I must have passed out before the helicopter came because the rest is a blur. You probably have a better sense of what happened after that."

Did he ever. Imagining the worst, he had rushed to the hospital, only to discover that Tacy's dad had gotten there first.

A fist against the window interrupted his musings. The deputy had finished removing the snake and was pantomiming his desire to be on his way. Seb wasn't about to let him leave without making sure the police department took this seriously. No matter what Tacy said, he still believed the snake had been placed into her car deliberately.

"I'll see what I can find out about the rattler, and then maybe we can continue our talk."

"Seb, I wish I could. But I texted my grandfather before I left the clinic and told him I'd be right home. I'm late enough already."

"Maybe this evening, then?" Did his voice sound as desperate as he felt? They had barely scratched the surface of what happened after the accident.

"I'm sorry, but I can't. Lois is making dinner, and then I need have that letter I have to read to my grandfather from my dad."

So, that was it then. Less than a couple of minutes of hazy recollections. No explanation. No closure. Disappointment whipped through his senses.

"Thanks again for everything, Seb."

She turned and slid around out the door.

"Glad I could help," he said. But Tacy was already gone. A moment later, her Nissan pulled out of the lot.

He stepped out of the truck and wandered over to the back of the police cruiser. On the ground next to the trunk was a large metal cage. Inside, the rattler had curled its long, thick body into a tight figure eight with its head tucked under its tail.

The deputy sidled up next to him. "It's quite a magnificent specimen. I'm no expert, but its scales and markings seem too pristine for it to have lived in the wild. It may sound crazy, but it looks like someone's pet."

It didn't sound crazy at all. It was just as he'd suspected. The snake hadn't fallen from a tree into Tacy's car. Someone had deliberately put it there. Someone who was targeting Tacy.

THREE

Tacy's mind was racing as she executed a sharp turn onto the road back to her grandfather's ranch. She had been surprised when Seb wanted to discuss the details of the accident. She had closed the book on that particular chapter of her life, and she had been glad to have a ready excuse to end the conversation. Still, it was strange to think that if Seb hadn't abandoned her that day at the hospital, he might have found out about her pregnancy before she did. As it was, she had woken up from her coma to the whispers of the doctors and nurses gathered by her bed.

"What a blessing that the baby survived the fall!"

"Baby! What baby?"

Her father had been the one to explain. She had sustained a serious concussion, broken both of her legs…and she was a week pregnant. Of course, her dad blamed Seb for everything, even though she repeatedly told him that he was being unfair. Seb hadn't tricked her into getting married. He hadn't bullied her into making the climb. He hadn't caused the fall. A firestorm of memories raged in her brain. The sneaking around, the secret engagement. The elopement. She and Seb had been in love, and nothing could change that. Not their age. Not their parents. And, most of all, not the feud.

Naturally, the fallout from the accident had exacerbated the enmity between their families. Her grandfather reneged on a previous agreement to lease water rights to the Hunts. The Hunts retaliated with a lawsuit. And her dad made the decision that they should move away.

Even though that was all years in the past, she knew she'd probably spend the next six months analyzing every single word Seb had uttered during their brief conversation in his truck today. It was certainly true that there were questions she wanted to ask him as well. Like why he left and never returned. And why he had never tried to contact her, not even when he filed for a divorce.

But right now, she had a more pressing concern. She needed to mentally prepare herself to read her grandfather the letter and to pray that it would mend the breach that her father had caused when he left. But when she got back to the ranch and looked in her suitcase, the letter wasn't there.

She searched for an hour before Lois called her down to dinner and then spent most of the meal trying to jog her memory by picturing the envelope with her dad's neat handwriting scrawled across the front. *For Carl Tolbert, to be read by Tacy Tolbert at Keith Tolbert's request.* In her mind's eye, she traced the script with her finger and touched the smooth sealed flap with her hand.

Her trick worked. She had a sudden recollection of slipping it in a bag with her cosmetics before coming to the ranch and then, earlier that morning before she went out on the ATV, she had taken it out of her cosmetic bag and placed it into the zippered compartment of her suitcase. She had already checked there twice, but it was worth another look.

She excused herself from the table and ran up to the room. Her fingers fumbled with the zipper to open the flap. But, no. The letter wasn't there. She blinked back tears of disappointment and frustration. She needed fresh air and a change of scenery to help her think.

Her thoughts flashed to the blue bicycle she had seen hanging in the garage. An invigorating ride would go a long way toward clearing her head. She just needed to offer her excuses to her grandfather and Lois, and then she could be on her way.

She found the two of them in the family room watching the news.

"Is everything okay, dear?" Lois hit the mute button and reestablished her grip on her grandfather's hand.

"Not really. I can't find my dad's letter."

Her grandfather frowned. "We thought that something was wrong when we heard you crashing around upstairs. But don't worry—it'll turn up. It's not the end of the world if you can't find it tonight."

"But I'm leaving tomorrow."

Her grandfather's face crumpled. "What?"

"I'm sorry. I knew that this wasn't the best time for a long visit, but I wanted to come now because I promised Dad that I wouldn't put off reading you his letter." She frowned. "I just can't imagine where it could have gone. I'm thinking of taking my old bike out for ride, hoping clearing my head will help me remember where I put the envelope."

"These are your last couple of hours here, and you're going for a bike ride?" Her grandfather seemed irritated at the thought. "It's getting dark."

"I'll wear the helmet and the reflector vest in the garage. I'll just go a few miles down County

Road 82 and turn back before I get to the junction."

Lois's phone rang in her pocket, and she pulled it out to check the screen. "Sorry. I need to take this," she said. With her cell to her ear, she walked into the hall.

Her grandfather shook his head. "It just doesn't seem like a good idea to go out this late, but I guess if you…"

Tacy was halfway out the door. "I'll be back before you know it." She made a beeline toward the battered blue three-speed hooked on the wall. It was a lot less sleek than the bike she rode in Denver, but it had the appeal of a familiar old friend. She pumped some air into the tires, slipped on the fluorescent vest, and slung her backpack over her shoulder. Then she pushed off down the driveway, pedaling slowly until she grew accustomed to the gears.

As soon she made the turn onto the road, her thoughts returned to the letter.

She felt reasonably certain that, once she had put it into the zippered pouch, she hadn't moved it again. Which led to the conclusion that someone had taken it. Lois? It was possible, especially if Seb was right about her putting drugs in the coffee.

But she could hardly confront Lois and accuse her of theft. No. When she got back to the ranch, she'd do another sweep of her room and the car. But if she came up short once again, she'd have to accept the fact that the letter was gone. If only she had opened the envelope when her dad handed it to her—then she could at least tell her grandfather what it said. But her dad had been adamant. She shouldn't read the letter until she arrived at the ranch.

Her eyes swept across the cliffs to take in the majestic reds of the sunset. God's country, her dad always called it. When the ranch was sold, her yearning for what was lost would be the same as her father's. Maybe even more so, since she had denied this legacy to her son.

Timmy. His name filled her mind as the vroom of a motor sounded behind her. She steered toward the shoulder, her wheels bumping along the loose gravel, providing ample room for the approaching car to pass. But rather than going around, the vehicle seemed to come up behind her. She could feel the heat from the hood, hear the roar of the engine. She pedaled faster. *Is it possible that the driver doesn't see me?*

Thunk. A bumper nudged against her back wheel, pushing her further off the road. She gripped the handlebars and pumped her legs as the bike careened forward from the impact.

The bike wobbled. Teetered. Her hands shook

as she squeezed hard on the brakes, struggling to regain control. She bumped along, and, after a few seconds, slowed to a stop. Her arms shook like jelly, and her heart thudded in her chest. But she hadn't fallen, and the bike was still in one piece.

She looked up at the turn in the road. The vehicle that hit her had disappeared in a cloud of dust. Could Seb be right? Was someone trying to kill her? She took a steadying breath. It didn't matter. She was leaving in the morning. Or… A thought occurred. She could make her excuses and leave tonight. She just needed to get back to the ranch and pack her stuff. Which might be harder than she thought since she was at least two miles away and the sky was getting darker every minute she delayed.

She unsnapped the clip on her helmet and climbed down to assess the damage. The tire wasn't punctured, but her back wheel was bent, which would make for a bumpy ride home. She turned the bike around and climbed on board just as a cacophony of sounds split the air. The hiss of tires on asphalt. The thumping drone of an engine accelerating into a turn. *Is the car coming back?* Her pulse accelerated. She didn't wait to turn and look. She pushed off, settling her feet against the pedals, and pumped her legs. She surged forward, but before she could steer off the road, the car hit her again from behind. A jolt of pain exploded in her leg. She hit the ground and rolled against the gravel as her breath jerked out in panicked gasps.

She raised her head and looked up just as red taillights disappeared in the distance. Whoever had hit her was gone. For now. She laid her head back down and gulped in air. The tears that had been pricking at the corners of her eyes rolled down her face.

With a groan, she rolled onto her back and pulled herself to a sitting position. Her head was throbbing, but when she removed her helmet and patted her hair, there was no wetness to indicate blood. Her elbows and legs were scraped and sore, but nothing seemed broken. She bent her hands against the ground and pushed up.

"Yow!" she howled. Sharp pain erupted from her ankle. She collapsed back onto the ground. A sob of despair shook her body. She was only a few yards from the side of the road. If she could maneuver her body closer, surely someone would drive by and help her.

Or…wait. Her phone was in her backpack, and her backpack was… Her eyes searched the ground next to her mangled bike, but she couldn't see it anywhere. If she could pull herself up on the shoulder, she'd have a better view.

She put her arms behind her and pushed,

scooting forward a few inches. Each time she moved, an agonizing pain ricocheted from her ankle up to her knee. Then again, the screws and plates that the doctors had put in after the accident did have a tendency to throb at the slightest provocation.

Slowly, carefully, she persisted, inching forward. By the time she reached the road, her hair was damp with perspiration and her arms were shaking. Pain was making her head swim, and she couldn't stop shivering. She wanted to be calm, rational, but the longer she stayed out there—frightened and in pain—the harder it became to think past her panic. And her strongest worry was not for herself but for her son. With the swelling and throbbing in her ankle, there was no way that she would be able to drive tomorrow to pick Timmy up at camp.

Her tears turned to sobs, so fierce that she was choking on them—and the familiar feeling of not being able to breathe caused her to hyperventilate. She was having a panic attack and losing her grip.

What was going to happen to her baby? Timmy had been through so much already. Her father's illness and sudden death had taken their toll on his once-cheerful nature. At one point, she even considered arranging for him to see a counselor to discuss his feelings. She had already sprung a big change on him when she signed him up for camp, but Timmy, being Timmy, had rolled with it. But what would he think if she didn't arrive to pick him up? What could he think? That his mom had forgotten him? That his mom didn't care?

Tires skidded on the shoulder behind her.

"Tacy! Are you okay? What happened?"

Steven Hunt.

She raised her eyes to look at him, but she couldn't find the words to explain.

"I'm calling 911. Hang in there, Tace."

Steven sounded panicked. Probably because she looked a mess. Her face felt sore and puffy, which meant that it had already started to swell. And her clothes were bloodied and covered with dirt. Steven lowered his voice as he spoke into his phone, but she couldn't summon the energy to listen in. Her breaths were coming in giant gulps. And all she could think about was Timmy, and making sure someone would be there to pick him up—that he'd be safe.

"Tacy? Tacy?" Steven bent down and knelt beside her. "Can you talk? The ambulance is on the way. Did you see what happened?"

"No, but…"

Timmy needed to be safe—needed to be picked up by someone she could trust to protect him. Whatever was behind this bizarre danger that surrounded her, she couldn't allow it to touch her son. And she trusted Steven. Trusted both the Hunt brothers, no matter what her family had always said.

Her dad had warned her of what would happen if the Hunts found out about Timmy. There would be lawyers involved and demands for shared custody. Her son would be sent off to spend summers at the ranch. But that worry suddenly felt small and distant. Timmy's safety was the only thing that truly mattered right now.

And maybe she could still protect her secret, too. Timmy was small for his age, so Steven wouldn't do the math and arrive at the logical conclusion that this was his nephew. She would call the camp and ask them to release her son to Steven. Meanwhile, she'd make arrangement for a flight home to Denver just in case she was too banged up to drive.

"Steven," she said. Her tongue felt thick and heavy and she could hear the way her words slurred. It was a struggle to get them out. "Help me. Please."

"Sure. Anything. What do you need, Tace?"

"Timmy," she said.

"Timmy? Who's Timmy?"

"Timmy. He's at…camp. In Wyoming. Pickup is…tomorrow. Ten."

"Who's this again?" Steven asked.

"Check my…my backpack. Camp brochure. Can you do this for me? Please? Find…" She swiveled her head around toward her bike. "Find my backpack."

"I think it would be better if I stayed right here until the ambulance arrives."

"No." Why couldn't she make him understand? What she was asking was more important. "Just look for my backpack. Tan. Black straps." She was crying in earnest now.

Steven stood up and walked toward her bike. *Please, God. Let him find it. Please.* She could feel blood drumming in her head as shock threatened to overwhelm her. But she needed to stay conscious, at least until Steven found her backpack.

The wail of sirens filled the air. *Hurry, Steven. Hurry.*

"Camp… Evergreen," she called out, not worrying about giving him an address or directions—all that information was in the brochure. "Tomorrow morning. Pick up Timmy."

"Right," Steven said.

"By ten o'clock." She closed her eyes. Steven would take care of it. He would follow the map and find the camp.

A second vehicle skidded to a stop on the side of the road.

A familiar face spun before her. "Seb." Was

that her voice? It felt so disconnected. "Steven's here. He's helping." She tried to gesture toward the spot where Steven was rifling through her backpack.

"Found it!" Steven yelled. He walked back to stand beside her, her backpack gripped in his hand.

Seb crouched next to her on the ground. "What happened?"

"The ambulance is here," Steven said as the rescue vehicle pulled in front of them, its lights flashing and its siren wailing.

She looked at Steven. "Don't tell anyone," she said.

"Tell anyone what?" Seb asked.

She met and held Steven's eyes as he slipped the brochure into the pocket of his jeans. She saw him nod once, slow and solemn. And then she allowed the blackness to engulf her.

"Hey. Steven. It's nine a.m., and I'm still at the hospital with Tacy. I don't know if you're getting my messages, but we need to talk about last night. I never got the full story of what happened out there on the road. As soon as you get this, call me back right away."

Seb slipped his phone back into his pocket and stretched out on the rickety folding chair he had positioned next to the bed. Tacy hadn't stirred since the nurse gave her a sedative sometime close to midnight. Her countenance, now so relaxed and serene, offered a marked change from the panic that had etched her features the night before.

Someone banged into a cart outside in the hall.

Tacy's eyes flickered open and darted around the room.

"Seb," she said when her eyes landed on him. "How long have I been sleeping?" Her eyes flicked over to the window, taking in the sunlight. "Have I been here all night?"

"Hi." He smiled down at her. "I'm glad you're finally awake. Are you feeling okay?"

"My ankle hurts, but not nearly as bad as it did last night. Did somebody contact my grandfather and tell him about the accident?"

"I did. I talked to Lois. She said that Carl would come by for a visit in the morning."

"A visit? No. But maybe he can give me a ride back to the ranch." Her eyes flickered back and forth across the room. "I remember Steven found my backpack in the ditch. Do you know where it ended up?"

He opened the drawer on the side of the bed. "He handed it to me before we left in the ambulance. I put it in here for safekeeping."

She snatched it from his hand, reached inside

and pulled out her phone. "Thanks. I just need to check and find out if…" Her voice trailed off as she scrolled through her messages. "Have you heard anything from Steven this morning?"

Steven? Why was she asking about Steven? Was it about the odd exchange that he'd overheard while they were waiting for the ambulance on the side of the road?

"No. But I've called him three times and texted a half-dozen messages."

"Why?" Her eyes drifted back to the screen of her phone.

"What do you mean, why? He was the first one on the scene, so I was hoping he could tell me what happened. But now that you're awake, maybe I should just ask you."

"I don't know, Seb. A car came up behind me and bumped me off the shoulder. I didn't see anything, not even the plates."

What? "I thought you crashed your bike. No one said anything about a hit-and-run."

Tacy didn't answer. She was typing on her phone.

"Can you wait on that for a minute, Tace? This is important."

She lifted her eyes for a moment, then went back to her text. "I'm listening," she said.

It sure didn't look like it.

"Did the driver notice that you had gone off the road?"

Her fingers froze on the screen. "I'm pretty sure he did since he turned around and rammed me again."

Tacy was hit twice? Seb blew out a long breath and tried to tamp down his impatience at her nonchalance—but it was difficult. She needed to take this more seriously. Why hadn't she told him that last night when he might still have been able to do something about it? More than ten hours had passed since the incident, and no one had made a move to secure the scene or search for evidence.

"Tace. If what you say is true, we're talking about attempted murder. You need to report this immediately. After everything else that happened yesterday, it seems clear that someone wants you dead."

"It wasn't Lois, if that was what you're thinking. She was home with my grandfather when I left on my bike."

"Are you sure she stayed put?"

Tacy's phone rang. She winced as she angled her body toward the window, cradling the receiver close to her ear. "Hi… Yeah. Good, thanks… Listen, it's fine. He has my approval… Okay. Great. Right. Thanks so much."

She ended the connection and turned back to face him.

"What?" she said.

"How can you be sure that Lois didn't make some excuse to leave the house once you left?"

"I can't. But I'll ask my grandfather when I see him. Okay?"

"Okay. But no matter what, you need to report the incident."

Tacy shrugged. "I guess."

She guessed? *What is going on?* It was almost as if her brain hadn't registered a single thing he had said. As if her mind was focused on something else entirely.

She seemed distracted. Worried—but not about this, which made no sense to him. What could possibly be more important than three near-death "accidents"?

Tacy glanced back down at her phone and then up at him again. "I plan to be back at the ranch in an hour or two, and I'll find out then if Lois left last night. But I'm still hoping to head home before dark."

A pang of disbelief shot across his brain. Did Tracy think that running away would erase the danger? "Someone tried to kill you, and you can't pretend it didn't happen and walk away. Besides, I assume the doctor isn't planning to release you at least until the end of the day."

"Then I'll check myself out. I know my rights. They can't keep me if I refuse to stay."

Someone shouted in the hall. A second later, Carl Tolbert stormed through the open door. "Tacy!" he said. "What has happened to you now? I knew I shouldn't let you go out on that dilapidated old bike."

"I'm fine, Grandfather. Just a little banged up. And now that you're here, I'm ready to go. I'm sure Seb's anxious to leave, too—he stayed with me last night, so he didn't get much sleep."

Is this a joke? Seb met and held Tacy's stare until she broke the connection and looked at her grandfather.

Uh-uh. She wasn't going to get rid of him that easily. "Thanks for looking out for my welfare, Tacy, but I think I might just stick around for a bit, at least until we call the sheriff. I'd feel better knowing that he was planning to send someone out to check the scene for evidence. You know. Leave no stone unturned, even when you're faced with a mountain of rocks."

He actually thought this might be one thing he and Carl might agree on—that they should do whatever it took to make sure Tacy was safe. But it seemed that hatred of Hunts still trumped everything else. Carl was glaring at him, and his finger was pointing straight at the door.

"You heard what my granddaughter said. She

wants you to leave. This is a family matter, and we don't need your help handling it."

This whole thing was getting more absurd by the minute. It was a typical Tolbert move to burst in and take charge without knowing any of the particulars. No wonder his parents kept hitting a wall in their attempts to negotiate water rights to the stream. Apparently, once Carl made up his mind about something, there was no changing it, no matter what the circumstances.

A weird sense of déjà vu played across his brain. In the hospital ten years ago, it had been Keith Tolbert issuing the orders and making the demands. But Seb was no longer that same guilt-ridden nineteen-year-old kid. And with Tacy's safety on the line, he wasn't going to back down so easily.

"I'll go if you want me to," he said, focusing just on her, "but before I leave, I want you to explain to your grandfather what happened last night. He needs to hear about the stampede and the rattler. And now this. I'm sure he'll be interested in learning more about the vehicle that almost…"

"I'll take care of it, Seb. I told you I would." Tacy pushed herself up on the bed. "I appreciate your assistance, I really do. But my grandfather's here now, and we have the situation under control."

She appreciates my assistance? The opposite seemed much closer to the truth. A slow burn of anger pulsed through his veins. She didn't need him now, and she hadn't needed him ten years ago. The sooner he accepted that, the better.

He pushed the door open, still chafing from the sting of Tacy's dismissal. He half expected that she might call him back to apologize. But that didn't happen. Her attention was once again firmly fixed on her phone. He reached into his pocket to pull out his keys, stopping short as he remembered that he had left his truck at the site of the accident. It was probably still there, unless Steven had seen fit to move it.

He pulled out his phone and checked for messages.

Nothing.

He'd hitch a ride back to his truck and then track down Steven. He needed to find some answers to the questions clamoring in his brain.

What did his brother know about the accident?

And what had Steven and Tacy been talking about that she wanted him to keep to himself?

FOUR

Tacy blinked up at the doctor, standing by her bed. According to the X-rays, her ankle wasn't broken. Her injury was nothing but a minor sprain. The hysteria she had experienced after the accident had been an overreaction, caused by anxiety and stress. And overwhelming worries about Timmy.

It had been a huge mistake to ask Steven to pick her son up at camp. But it was too late to stop him. She glanced at the clock above the television. Ten thirty. He should already be on his way home.

"Tacy!" Her grandfather's sharp voice brought her back to the present. "Did you hear what the doctor just said? You need to make sure that you take it easy and not overdo it."

"What?" She forced a smile. "Sorry. Yes, of course."

"Humph." Her grandfather snorted. He fixed his gaze on the bespectacled doctor who had moved across the room and was now standing by the door. "Can I talk to you a minute in the hall?"

"Sure," the doctor said. As the door swung shut behind the two men, Tacy grabbed her phone and tapped out a text to Steven. Where are you? She waited a moment, but when a reply wasn't immediate, she threw on her clothes and signed the insurance papers. Ten minutes later, she was climbing into the back seat of her grandfather's truck and propping up her leg.

"Everything okay back there?" Her grandfather's voice sounded weary as he headed out of the lot.

"Yes. Of course. I didn't mean to worry you. You must have wondered what happened when I didn't return from the bike ride. I hope that Lois was with you, so you didn't have to fret on your own."

"I wanted to go out and look for you, but I had no idea which way you went. We paced the floor for hours, waiting for you to come home. Finally, Lois gave me a sleeping pill and sent me to bed. I was glad she had good news to share in the morning."

"I'm so sorry that I caused you so much concern."

"What are you apologizing for?" He glared at her through the rearview mirror. "This isn't your fault. But we do need to get to the bottom of what happened out there on the road. And all those other things that Hunt boy mentioned."

She closed her eyes. Her grandfather was right about the need to investigate the hit-and-run, especially if it was connected to her other accidents. The driver of the car that ran her down was aiming to kill her, of that she was sure. She took a deep breath and clenched her hands to keep them from shaking. She needed to get out of here—the hospital, Chimney Bluff, the state of North Dakota—and fast. But all she could think about was Steven, sitting in the car with Timmy. Would he figure it out? Her phone buzzed in her pocket. She pulled it out and scanned the screen. Picked up TT. Not what I was expecting. Can't wait to hear what you have to say. Should arrive back in 45 min.

Her heart skipped a beat. What did he know?

"Looks like Lois isn't home yet," her grandfather said. She realized with a start that they were pulling into the driveway. "Though I figure you wouldn't want her fussin' over you anyway."

Tacy nodded as she slid out of the car. She certainly did not want anyone fussing over her, especially not Lois, if there was any chance that she might have actually put something dangerous in the coffee. But then, her grandfather had confirmed that Lois couldn't have been the driver that hit her the previous night. Did that mean Lois was innocent after all? Tacy didn't know what to believe—and she couldn't concentrate on anything but the thought of her son.

She faked a yawn. "I am feeling tired, though. I think I'll go upstairs and get some sleep."

"Good idea. I might take a nap, too, but if you need anything, come and get me immediately."

She followed her grandfather into the house and up the stairs, her fingers reaching for her phone before she even closed the guest room door.

Steven picked up on the second ring. "Well, hiya, Tace. Been expecting to hear from you for a while now."

"Oh, Steven. Thank you so much for getting Timmy. Can I talk to him for a minute?"

Her son's high voice piped in. "Hi, Mom," he said.

She choked back tears. "Hi, baby. Sorry that I couldn't be there to get you at camp, but I'll see you really, really soon."

"That's okay. Steven's nice. Did you know that his family just got a new puppy named Cody?"

"I didn't, but..."

"Me, again, Tace." Steven's voice came back on the line, with a hint of something steely in his undertone that she couldn't quite identify. "Is there maybe something you want to tell me?"

"Huh? No. I mean, yes. We have to figure out where we can meet. I'm out of the hospital and back at my grandfather's ranch, so why don't I meet you at the Red Robin off the interstate? I can buy you a late lunch. And then Timmy and I can hit the road."

"Actually, I picked up some snacks on my way to the camp, so nah, we're not hungry. I guess we need to come up with a new plan."

She suppressed a sigh. Trust Steven to be difficult. "Okay. How about we meet at your parents' old bunkhouse in about thirty minutes?"

"That'll work. I've been using the place as an office, so, yeah, we can make the exchange there. But it seems like kind of an odd meeting place. Like maybe you have something you want to hide."

Well, he wasn't wrong—but she'd go with the truth that was easier to share. "My grandfather doesn't know about Timmy. My dad never said so in so many words, but I think he was afraid that the news might cause my grandfather to get his hopes up about a reconciliation."

"Your grandfather? Right. I think maybe there are a few *other* people that you forgot to tell as well."

Her heart was pounding. *He knows.*

"I'll see you in a half an hour," Steven said. "But use that time well. Because if you don't tell Seb, I will. And I think it might go down better coming from you."

Click.

Her heart pounded a staccato rhythm in her chest. The next move was hers. The simplest option would be to tell Seb about Timmy and face the consequences. Over the last twenty-four hours, he had proven to be steadfast and protective. And even in her lowest moments, stewing in hurt and a sense of betrayal, she'd never thought Seb was a cruel or vicious man. She wasn't sure she could rely on him, but she knew he'd never harm her—or their child. But she couldn't forget that he had abandoned her ten years ago at the first bump in the road.

On the other hand, time seemed to have matured him, and Timmy deserved a father.

The stakes were so high. She didn't want to do anything that might risk upsetting her son. What would happen if she told Seb the truth? He would be angry. She'd be defensive. And Timmy would be stuck in the middle.

Okay. New plan. Her car was parked right at the front of the driveway, and it would take less than ten minutes to reach the bunkhouse. The hard part would be convincing Steven that this was the wrong time and place for a father/

son reunion. She felt she actually had a pretty strong case to make on that point. Considering the looming danger, it wasn't safe for Timmy to stay in Chimney Bluff, even for a short visit.

She glanced down at the pile of shirts and jeans on her bed. Usually when she packed, she folded her clothing into neat little piles. But there was no time for that now. She threw everything into her suitcase and closed it with a click. As she tiptoed down the stairs, her heart raced with anticipation. If she hurried, she ought to arrive at the bunkhouse before Steven.

She turned down the dusty track that led to the small log structure that once had been the favorite hideout for her, Seb and Steven. The dirt road passed directly in front of the main house, and a rush of wariness pulsed through her veins. Even after all of this time, it was still disconcerting to be on Hunt property. As a teenager, she had never taken this route. It had been quicker—and sneakier—to cut directly through the pasture. She could feel her lips turn up in a wistful smile. A lot of good it had done keeping her friendship with the Hunt boys a secret. But at the time, it had been the three of them against the world. Or, at the very least, against their parents and their unreasonable feud. *Tolberts don't associate with Hunts*. That was the line that had been drilled into her head for as long as she could remember.

The bunkhouse came into view, sheltered in a grove of thick pines. It looked like she was the first to arrive. *Good.* She climbed out of her car and made her way slowly up the steps to the porch. The door was open, so she stepped inside.

The place was exactly as she remembered it. The galley kitchen where they used to make sandwiches and heat frozen pizza. The bright yellow curtains and the threadbare rug on the floor. The two bedrooms off the main hall. The bookshelf filled with Hardy Boys and Nancy Drew paperbacks. Steven had claimed to be using it as an office, but the only evidence of that was a stack of papers on the counter by the stove and an open computer on the desk.

At the sound of a motor, her heart fluttered in her chest. Timmy. At last.

The door creaked open.

Her heart dropped. It was Seb.

"So, you did manage to talk your way out of the hospital. I should have known you'd find a way to do that. But I thought you'd be resting back at your grandfather's. What are you doing here?"

Dread swamped her body. "I was wondering the same thing about you."

"I'm looking for Steven."

"Well, as you can see, he's not here. Maybe you should check the stables."

"Already have."

"What about Dot's Diner? He could be having a late lunch."

Seb took another step into the room. "Why are *you* here, again?"

She said the first thing she could think of. "I wanted to see this place before I took off. It sure brings back a lot of memories."

"Okay." His raised brow hinted that he didn't quite believe her. "Did you remember to ask your grandfather if Lois went out last night?"

"I did. He said that she was with him, waiting for me to return." She glanced down at her watch, then fidgeted anxiously, wincing at the burst of pain from her ankle. "Say, Seb. I know that this is going sound weird, but would you mind giving me a little time here by myself?"

He stared at her for a minute. "You need time to yourself in my family's bunkhouse?" He didn't wait for her reply. "Okay. Sure. We can talk later. I assume you plan to stick around for a bit. Maybe I'll walk to the barn and recheck the stables. Never know. Steven might be back."

He turned away from her and walked across the room. The door swished shut behind him. A minute later, gravel crunched on the driveway.

Tacy limped out to the porch as a tan truck ground to a stop in front of the bunkhouse.

Steven was at the wheel, and Timmy was next to him in the passenger seat. It had only been three days, but she felt a surge of joy at the sight of her son.

The driver's door opened, and Steven jumped out.

"Hi, Tace," he said.

"Hi," she whispered. Out of the corner of her eye, she could see Seb, halfway down on the path.

Thunk! Steven slammed the door.

Seb stopped in his tracks and spun around. He raised his hand up and waved. Then he turned and began walking back to join them.

Tacy fixed her eyes on Timmy, who hadn't moved from his seat. She waved her hand to get his attention, but he didn't look up. Did he even realize that the truck had stopped? Maybe not if he was lost playing FreeCell on Steven's phone.

"Isn't this nice?" Steven said with a smile. "Looks like the gang's all here. I've got to give it to you, Tace. I didn't think you'd do it, but I guess you told Seb after all."

Seb reached the top of the path and stepped between them. "Told me what?"

Tacy's eyes darted between Steven and Seb.

"Told me what?" Seb asked again as the passenger door opened and Timmy catapulted out of the truck.

"Hi, Mom," he said.

Her heart lurched. Side by side, Timmy and Seb looked like the before-and-after photos of a time traveler's journey over twenty years. The shape of their faces, the tilt of their chins. The two of them even had the same broad smile, although no one was smiling at the moment. Not even Timmy.

Especially not Timmy. Her baby was always so perceptive, so quick to pick up on the tension in any room.

"Mom? What's going on?" Timmy's bottom lip trembled.

"It's all good, Timmy," she said. She pulled her son to her and considered her chances of evasion or escape.

Did Seb realize Timmy was his son? Guessing from the look on his face, she'd say yes. Did Timmy realize that Seb was his dad? Not yet. And, at least for the moment, she'd like to keep it that way.

"Timmy," she said, stepping back from the embrace. "Did Steven tell you that I asked him to pick you from camp because I hurt my leg?"

"Yeah." Timmy nodded. "He said that you would meet us at his parents' ranch. He said that he was an old friend of yours and that you both grew up around here."

"I told you about it. Remember? When Gramps was so sick and we were talking about what it was like when we lived in North Dakota? Well, this is the place."

"Okay. But do you think we can start to drive home tonight? I have baseball tryouts next week, and the coach said we shouldn't miss."

Right. She had made a note of the time and location on her calendar at home. Bredesen Field. Two o'clock, Thursday.

"We'll definitely be home by then."

Steven pulled out his truck keys and tossed them in the air. "Hey, buddy. I know you want to get going, but what do you say I give you the grand tour of the family ranch? I'll show you the lake where I almost drowned when I was just your age. And we can stop by the house and you can meet our new puppy. And we can grab a big handful of my mom's famous chocolate chip cookies. They're good enough to make you forget about baseball. All you'll care about is going back for more."

Tacy blew a short breath out of her nose. She had to hand it to Steven. He had managed to lob two grenades with one toss. The first, a subtle reminder of Timmy's age, just in case Seb hadn't been paying attention. And the second, an unscheduled stop into Sandy Hunt's kitchen. That one needed to be nipped in the bud immediately.

"Thanks for the offer, Steven, but if you don't mind, I think Timmy should skip the cookies. He and I will probably stop and get something to eat on the road, so I'd rather not spoil his appetite for dinner."

"Aww, Mom." Timmy frowned. That boy sure did love dogs and chocolate chip cookies.

Steven's eyes were on her, but his words were directed toward Timmy. "Your mom's the one in charge here, not me. Let's go visit the buffalo instead. We can climb up and watch them from the top of the gate."

"Awesome. Mom, is that okay?"

"Yes. Just be careful," she said. But Timmy and Steven were already halfway down the path.

She took a deep breath and forced herself to look at Seb.

For a long moment, he was silent. But the expression in his eyes… She didn't have to ask if he'd put the pieces together. She knew he had.

"What did you tell him about me?" he asked.

"I told him that his dad was in the military. I said that it was hard for him to take care of us, being so busy defending our country. It sounds lame when I say it now, but he understood."

"*He understood?* Says who? I guarantee that he had—and still has—a lot of issues with that."

"Maybe. But my dad and I decided that the truth could wait."

Seb clenched his fingers into a tight fist. "I should have known that Keith was the mastermind of this deception. That's why he made you move away, wasn't it? He wanted to keep my kid all to himself." He tensed, forcing out the next question between clenched teeth. "Or did he take his anger out on Timmy? Did he blame him for being half Hunt?"

"Of course not. He wasn't happy when he found out I was pregnant. How could he be? But he loved Timmy. It would have been hard not to. He was such a sweet baby that..."

"Let's skip the memories of the early years. I missed all that, in case you don't remember. Tell me something, Tacy. Did you and your dad ever even think of all the people who were affected by your decision? Me. My mom and dad. Steven. Though I guess I shouldn't worry about him too much since he knew about Timmy before I did."

"Seb. I had to tell Steven. Last night, I thought my ankle might be broken. I knew I couldn't drive. I needed someone to pick him up at camp."

"Right. And it wouldn't make sense to ask his father."

His father. After so many years of denying the truth, those words struck a chord in her heart. "I thought about it. But I couldn't. Seb, I'm sorry. You have to understand."

"Why don't you be the one who tries to understand? In case you forgot, someone has been trying to kill you since you arrived in town. I've been tearing my hair out trying to get you to recognize the danger—but at every step, you've been blowing me off. Making excuses. Staring at your phone. I thought you were ignoring me, but you weren't. You were focusing on Timmy instead. On how to keep your secret instead of keeping yourself and *our son* safe. There were two of you I should have been worrying about all this time, and I never even knew. Because instead of telling me about Timmy so I'd be prepared just in case, you held on to your secret and hoped for the best. You've got to admit that was a pretty dumb strategy."

"I'll admit nothing of the kind. You show up in my life again after ten years and I'm supposed to just pour out all my troubles on your shoulders? Why on earth would I trust you with any of that? You left me, remember?"

The memory of the brokenness she had felt when she found out that Seb had gone back to

Texas after her accident was as real to her now as it was back then. At first, she couldn't believe it. Seb had always been the one person she could rely on, the boy who would never let her down. But as the days passed, reality dawned. He wasn't coming back. He had left her, just like her mom did when she was eight. It felt as if someone had yanked her heart out of her chest.

He shook his head. "We both know who left—who moved away without looking back. I wrote you dozens of letters. And called at least a hundred times. How was I supposed to stay with someone who was already gone?"

What? That was news to her. She hadn't seen any letters or heard about any calls. In fact, there had been nothing but a wall of silence until Seb filed for divorce. And even that was a fuzzy memory—her dad handing her the paperwork and telling her to sign on the dotted line.

Were Seb's claims true? Her father was overprotective, but surely he wouldn't have gone that far. Or would he? She looked into Seb's eyes, which were heavy with disappointment, and was struck by the certainty that, regardless of what had happened between them, it had been wrong to keep Seb from his son. But that didn't mean that this was the right moment to tell Timmy the truth. She needed time. She needed space.

She needed to protect her son—not just from danger but from confusion and disappointment.

"I need to take Timmy home, Seb. You're the one who keeps telling me that it isn't safe for us to stay."

She walked back into the bunkhouse and sat down on a bed. Tears prickled the corners of her eyes, but she pushed them away with the back of her hand. For Timmy's sake, she needed to stay strong.

She reached into her pocket and pulled out her phone. There was no one to call, no one she wanted to talk to, but it was better to look busy than to let Seb see her cry.

Seb watched Tacy scroll through the messages on her cell. Her forehead was scrunched, and her eyes were cast downward, almost as if she thought he'd disappear if she refused to acknowledge his presence.

Sorry, but it wasn't going to work.

"Nope," he said.

She didn't look up, so he said it again.

"Nope. I know there's danger, but running from it isn't the answer. If you stay here, I can help you get to the bottom of what's going on. And at the same time, I can get to know my son. We don't have to tell him that I'm his dad. At least not right away. It might be awkward, but you can give your grandfather a heads-up about what's going on. And I'll do the same with my folks. I'll even make sure they don't ask Timmy to call them Grandma and Grandpa. But this will be a first step toward something more significant. You owe me this, Tacy. You owe it to all of us. You can move in here. I'll bring you some towels and fresh sheets. It'll feel just like home."

She shot him a look. "And how do you suggest I sell this to my grandfather? *I have a son I didn't tell you about. And by the way, we're both staying at the Hunts' bunkhouse.*"

He shrugged. "That sounds about right. I'll tell my mom to expect all of us for dinner. Fried chicken, okay? You can talk to her about the menu for the next couple of days."

"Let's not get carried away here. We have lives waiting for us at home. You heard Timmy. He wants to get back for baseball tryouts. He's not going to be happy to hear there's been a change of plans."

"That's right—you have lives. Lives that I should have been a part of all along. You've kept my son from me for almost ten years. I think I deserve more than five minutes with him before you walk away again. I am going to be a part of my son's life, Tacy. You might not like it, but that's the way it has to be. As far as baseball tryouts go, well… Eventually, you'll have to explain to him that I wasn't exactly the delinquent dad you painted me out to be. One of us is going to look bad, no matter how you play it. I've been the villain for ten years. Now it's your turn."

Harsh words. But he was determined to make up for lost time in the days ahead. And he couldn't ignore the excitement exploding in his chest. He had a son!

"Seb?" Tacy's tone was laced with frustration. "Are you forgetting that I'm in danger? You've convinced me that all of these incidents aren't accidents. That someone is trying to kill me. Would Timmy even be safe here?"

He rolled his head back on his neck. Tension was building in his head. What Tacy was saying was true. There was a threat against her. But he couldn't let this moment pass. He had already missed ten years of his son's life. He wasn't ready to say goodbye when he hadn't even had the chance to get to know Timmy. And what if the danger followed Tacy back to Colorado? At least here, he could protect her. He just had to make her understand.

"Tacy, going back to Denver doesn't guarantee you'll be safe. If trouble follows you, what then?"

That seemed to pull her up short. Seizing his advantage, he stepped forward. "Please, Tacy.

You can't tell me I have a son and then take him away where I can't see him. I admit that there is a risk in remaining here in Chimney Bluff, but there could be a risk in Colorado too. If you stay here, I'll do everything I can to protect you."

It was a big promise. But he was trained Army MP. He had kept witnesses safe before. He just needed to maintain a constant watch over the two of them. To always be on the lookout. To always be ready.

Tacy didn't look convinced. Not completely. But she didn't say no right away, either. He held his breath and waited. After a long beat of silence, her shoulders slumped.

"Okay," she whispered at last. "We'll stay, at least for a couple of days."

"Thank you," he whispered, flooded with relief so strong that his knees wobbled. He had a chance—to get to know his son, to build some kind of relationship.

And to make sure no one dared to harm this precious piece of his family he'd only just learned he had.

FIVE

A sharp pain shot up from Tacy's ankle as she lifted her suitcase from the trunk of her car. It hurt even more as she dragged her bag into the bunkhouse, her injured leg cramping and throbbing and slowing her gait. She fixed her lips into a stoic smile as she passed through the main room where Seb was waiting.

Of course, he had tried to lend a hand, following her out to her car and engaging in a mini-scuffle over the luggage. But she had shooed him away, insisting that she was perfectly capable of handling it herself.

Which she was. And she needed some time alone to think.

She never should have hidden her pregnancy from Seb. She had been wrong to allow her feelings of hurt and betrayal to color the choices she had made. But what about Seb's claim that he had tried to contact her after the accident? Could that be true? And if so, did it change anything? She wasn't sure. Her judgment had proven time and time again to be faulty. It was enough to have her second guessing every decision she'd made—including the one to stay in Chimney Bluff when someone was after her. Was she making the wrong decision again, putting not just herself but her son in harm's way?

There was a lot to consider as she made her way back and forth between her car, Steven's truck and the bunkhouse. Timmy's belongings were stuffed into a canvas duffel, along with all of his dirty clothes and half-finished craft projects from camp. Thankfully, instead of sulking about baseball tryouts, he had already begun to look upon the change in their plans as a great adventure. Apparently, Steven had taken advantage of their time in the car to regale him with stories of horses, rocky trails and herds of buffalo. So what if he didn't get the chance to try out for the traveling team? Baseball could wait until next year.

Tacy dragged her suitcase into the larger of the two rooms and heaved it onto a bed. The springs of the old mattress creaked under its weight, and a cloud of dust rose up in the air. She covered her mouth mid-sneeze. This place was going to wreak havoc with Timmy's allergies. Did she bring along an extra vial of his meds? She opened her cosmetic bag and looked inside. Nope. Another mistake. Then again, she hadn't expected that they were going to get stuck living in a musty old bunkhouse on the Hunt ranch.

She tossed her cosmetic bag onto the mattress. It missed and hit the floor.

"Mom?" Timmy's voice piped from the next room.

She stuck her head around the door. "No worries. I just dropped something onto the floor."

Her eyes moved to Seb, who was sitting next to him on the couch.

Seb set down his copy of *Field & Stream* and shot her a suspicious look. It was almost as if he thought that if he let her out of his sight, she might pack up Timmy and leave. Which was not to say that she wasn't tempted to do exactly that. But it would only exacerbate an already volatile situation. She just needed to buck up and accept that Seb was going to be part of their lives going forward whether she liked it or not.

As for the rest—facing the Hunts, telling her grandfather, figuring out a visitation schedule for Seb and Timmy—she'd just have to take it one day at a time, one hour at a time, really, because it wasn't going to be easy to make it through the evening. Once she finished unpacking, she and Timmy (and Seb, she supposed, since he seemed to be sticking to them like glue) would walk up to the main house for the big meet-and-greet with his parents, where they'd be forced to act like one big happy family.

Funny that. She used to dream of dinner at the Hunts' when she was a kid. She would imagine all the interesting conversations, the good-natured teasing, and the mouth-watering meals shared around the big oak table in the massive dining room at the back of the house. It was a world apart from supper in the kitchen with her dad and grandfather tossing barbs at each other, while passing around a take-and-bake casserole from the grocery store. Of course, the feud made it impossible for her to ever publicly associate with the Hunts. They were the enemy, never to be treated as friends. But she had never applied that rule to Seb and Steven.

Before anything else, she needed to change out of the clothes she had worn home from the hospital. She pushed aside the top items in her suitcase and dug deep to find a clean shirt and a fresh pair of jeans. Her fingers closed around a cotton cardigan as something soft moved against her skin. She pulled back her hand and looked down at a spider tiptoeing along her right arm.

Goose bumps pricked her flesh.

"Seb." Her voice wobbled somewhere between a scream and a gasp.

Boots pounded across the floor.

Seb stepped into the room. The color drained from his face as his eyes fixed on her out-stretched arm and the spider's long legs tapping against her skin. He took a step closer. "Looks like a black widow. Let me see if I see if I can coax it to move onto my hand."

"No," she whispered. But he didn't seem to hear. She held her breath as he placed his open palm onto the crook of her arm and waited. Time seemed to stop as the spider paused, its eight legs suddenly still. Her heart pounded, and a bead of sweat dropped from her forehead onto her frozen arm.

With his left hand, Seb reached for a paper-back book on the nightstand by the bed.

The black widow edged forward, consider-ing its options.

"C'mon, buddy. Climb on over," Seb said.

The spider flailed its antennae to test the new surface. It must have met with its approval be-cause it slowly crept across Seb's fingers and onto his palm.

He tilted his arm, nudging the creature to-ward the book he was holding in his other hand. It was slow going, but he didn't flinch. The quivering bulbous ball, with its small head and clicking mandibles, seemed to sense that things might end badly once it left the safety of his arm. But at last, it edged onto the cover of the paperback.

Seb moved quickly across the room and dropped the spider and book into the trash can. Then he grabbed the box of a board game from the bookshelf and slammed it on top.

She let out a long, broken breath. "Seb, I…" Her voice faltered, and her eyes filled with tears.

He handed her a handkerchief from the pocket of his jeans. "Hey, don't cry. You know I've always enjoyed playing with spiders."

She knew he was just trying to cheer her up, but in her current state of anxiety, she couldn't appreciate the joke. "How did a black widow get trapped inside my suitcase? And how long do you think it was there?"

"It's hard to say. Spiders can go quite a while without food and water."

She looked toward the door. *Timmy! What had he heard?*

Seb moved past her for a peek into the adjoining room. "Our boy seems to be fast asleep."

Our boy. It actually sounded kind of nice.

She looked at Seb. He hadn't hesitated to lure that wretched spider onto his arm. He had put her safety over his own. He had protected her from harm. Again. Because the harm…just seemed to keep coming.

"This wasn't an accident," she said.

He nodded. "I don't think so either."

"But why a spider? Who keeps something like that around just in case they need to scare someone half to death?"

Seb eyed the group around the dining room table—his folks, Tacy, Timmy and Steven. It was a gathering of those nearest and dearest to his heart.

But that didn't make it easy. The air conditioner was set to a cool sixty-six, but the emotional temperature of the room was a hundred degrees and rising. He squirmed in his seat, his eyes moving like a ping-pong ball between his mom and Tacy. The stress of the situation was clearly taking its toll on Tacy. Her mouth was drawn into a deep frown, and her eyes were edged with anxiety.

There were far too many long glances and raised eyebrows for his liking. Only Timmy seemed to be enjoying himself. At the very least, he was enjoying the food, reaching for a second helping of chicken and extra butter for his corn on the cob.

"Nice to see a young boy who likes his vegetables," his dad said. "I guess the apple doesn't fall far from the tree."

"Huh?" Timmy scrunched his eyes and turned toward his mother.

"It's just a saying, Timmy." Tacy flushed as she stared down at her plate.

It would have been a good time to change the subject. Instead, his mom ramped it up. "He looks just like you," she mouthed, tilting her head toward Timmy.

He shot a look in her direction. *Cease and desist immediately.*

Tacy's forced smile seemed to crumple around the edges each time the conversation trailed into difficult territory. Which seemed to happen every fifteen minutes. They'd be talking about the ranch, and all of a sudden, Timmy would say that he wanted to go riding. Or his mom would suggest that they all should drive together to the church picnic. And maybe Tacy could help her make pies for the bake sale. It was all too much, especially given the stress Tacy was under from the attacks. He needed to talk to his folks and clue them in about the danger.

He shifted his eyes to look at Timmy, who was now wearing a worried frown.

Tacy seemed to have noticed it too. "How are you doing, Timmy?" she asked.

"Good," he said. "I was just thinking about what the coach will say when I don't show up for tryouts."

Tacy reached over and squeezed Timmy's

hand. "I'll send him a text and explain what's going on. In the meantime, you need to remember that it's quite a bit different being on a ranch. There are lots of animals around, and though most of them are friendly, some might not like it if you get too close."

"I know that, Mom," Timmy said. "Steven told me all about the buffalo. If one comes near me, I know just what to do."

"What's that?" Tacy raised a brow.

"Find the nearest tree and climb it."

She bent over and kissed the top of his head. "That might work in an emergency, but you shouldn't go off exploring without one of us along."

Seb flinched as someone kicked him under the table. Steven. Apparently, his brother had been watching him watching Tacy. *Don't go there, bro,* Steven's eyes seemed to say.

Steven was right, of course. But still… He had been finding it hard to drag his gaze off Tacy.

His dad stood up from the table. "What do you say we all pitch in and haul some supplies to the bunkhouse?"

Together, they raided the linen closet and pantry. Snacks, bottles of water, towels, sheets and pillowcases were quickly loaded into everyone's arms. From the look of things, his folks seemed to be equipping their visitors for a lengthy stay. His dad handed a pillow and a blanket to Timmy, and they led the way back to the bunkhouse.

Seb's offer to help was summarily rejected. Fine. He'd give them a half an hour and then pop in to check their progress. In the meantime, he'd look for Steven in the barn with the horses.

The heady scent of sun-dried hay assailed his nostrils as he slid open the wide door. He took a deep breath to pull it all in, welcoming the familiar sensory overload.

Steven was standing next to one of the horse stalls, his foot propped against a rail. "Hey, bro. What's it like finding out you have a nine-year-old kid?"

"It's good. Especially knowing that you got to spend so much time with him before I even knew he existed."

A smile leaked from Steven's lips. "I like that part, too."

"I thought you would. I called you a couple times when Tacy and I got to the hospital. But apparently, you've forgotten how to answer your phone."

"I didn't return your messages because I didn't have anything to say—not to your questions, anyway. I didn't see the accident. All I remember is being passed by a silver sedan right before I saw Tacy on the side of the road."

"Okay, then." Seb turned and walked toward the door.

"Wait." Steven called after him. "Don't you want to know why?"

"Why, what?" He reached for the handle on the barn door, anxious to return to the bunkhouse.

But Steven's voice beckoned him back inside. "Don't you want to know why I was so distracted? I had just found out that Carl Tolbert rejected my bid and accepted someone else's offer on the ranch."

Seb walked across the barn and leaned against the stall next to his brother. Since retiring from the rodeo circuit, Steven had been chasing a dream to build a shelter for older bulls that were no longer able to compete. The Tolbert land would have been perfect, but now it looked like Steven and his consortium of investors would have to find somewhere else.

"Sorry, Steven. That's a tough break. Do you know who submitted the winning bid?"

"It's all hush-hush at this point in the game. This would go down easier if the whole process hadn't been so sketchy from the start. It's hard to point a finger at Carl, since he isn't really involved in the details of the sale. I considered asking Tacy to talk to him and see what she could find out. But I don't know that I trust her now that we know the big secret she kept hidden all this time. How could she keep you in the dark about the baby?"

Seb shrugged. If he could answer that question, he'd be a happier man. In any case, he appreciated his brother's loyalty.

"I've been wondering how all of this will affect that job you've been offered in DC."

"I've been thinking the same thing. I still have time to make a decision. But my main goal moving forward is to spend as much time as possible with my son." He looked at his watch. "I suppose I better head over to the bunkhouse to make sure Mom isn't asking for baby pictures of Timmy so she can compare them to mine."

"He does look a lot like you did back then. If hearing that makes Tacy uncomfortable, then so be it. I'd be inclined to say she has it coming."

"I get it. And I'm definitely still upset about how this whole thing played out. But there's not a lot I can do about it, though, except try to work through it so I can be part of Timmy's life. Holding grudges isn't going to help, especially when I know this isn't easy on Tacy, either. She still has to tell her grandfather about Timmy. Any way you look at it, that's bound to be a difficult conversation for both of them.

He's not going to like that she's staying here, but I don't think she'd be safe under his roof. She sure hasn't been so far."

Steven nodded. "Just let me know what I can do to provide protection. I got a look at Tacy's bike when I was searching for her backpack, and the frame was mangled beyond recognition. The driver of the car was trying to do more than scare her."

"I agree. Whoever's doing this is determined and serious. And with Timmy in the mix, we need to have eyes on both of them 24/7."

SIX

Seb met his mother halfway between the bunkhouse and the barn.

"We need at least another hour to get organized," she said. "I left your dad with Timmy and Tacy, and I'm headed back to the main house to get more cleaning supplies. The countertops are filthy, and the floor is covered with dust and grime."

"Yeah, well. This particular situation is a surprise for all of us. But I'm here to help. Tell me what to do."

"Honestly? The four of us are bumping into each other every time we turn around. Why don't you come back at seven? By then, we ought to have the situation under control."

He looked at his watch. "Okay. And, Mom? Thanks."

"That little boy is precious to us, too. I am thankful to God for this unexpected blessing."

Unexpected blessing. He wouldn't disagree with that.

"Quick question, Mom. I know you don't like to gossip, but is there anything you can tell me about Carl's new wife? I know she used to live in Reno, but that's about it."

"Hmm. I really haven't spent any time in her company. Initially, I thought she was avoiding me because of the feud, but from what I've heard, it's just her way. But, let me think." She pressed her lips together. "I do remember overhearing her ask one of the ladies if Chimney Bluff had a community theater. That's the best I can come up with at the moment."

"That's great. Thanks, Mom. I'm going inside to do work on my computer, but I'll see you back at the bunkhouse in an hour."

He went up to his room and sat down at his desk. Though he had never formally met Lois Tolbert, he had seen her at church and around town. She was a lot younger than Carl, a fact that had initially set tongues wagging. He tapped in a search for "community theater Reno" and garnered twelve legitimate hits. He opened the first and clicked through dozens of photos from past productions, but no one resembling Lois appeared in the cast. It was the same with the second and the third theater companies on the list. But when he tapped on the fourth, his fingers moved to zoom in on a photo from a production of *Oliver!* by the Merrywood Players. He scrolled to the bottom of the page to identify the cast member who had caught his eye. "In the role of Mrs. Corney is Lois Dill, third from the right." He pulled the image closer. The eyes and the shape of the face were definitely familiar, despite the heavy makeup and brown wig.

He had a new name. Lois Dill.

And, bingo! Seconds later, he had an address and an old newspaper article about a fire that destroyed the property at 220 Clearwater Lane. A Mr. Curtis Dill was home at the time. According to initial reports, the blaze was being investigated as arson.

There was something else in the article, too. Lois Dill's former residence was listed as Ocala, Florida. Which opened up a whole new line to his investigation.

A search of community theater in Ocala produced fewer results. Which made it easier to find another picture of Lois—this time, going by the name of Lois Evans—mugging to the camera in the role of Golde in *Fiddler on the Roof.* He followed that persona to a newspaper account of a fatal fishing accident that claimed the life of one of the town's most popular physicians, Dr. Charles Evans, who, along with his wife, Lois, had been trolling for grouper on the Gulf.

His breath hitched. Two husbands dead, with foul play suspected in the demise of at least one of them.

He paced around the room, but that didn't even begin to burn off his anxiety. He needed to talk to Tacy, but he didn't want to be in the way. He checked his watch. His mom said they needed an hour, but only forty-five minutes had passed. Close enough. He thudded down the stairs and out the door, his steps hastening across the yard. He needed to get back to Tacy's side.

He walked into the bunkhouse and headed into the small bedroom just in time to see Tacy tucking a thin cotton blanket around Timmy's shoulders. One look at her strained face, and he got the message. She was overwhelmed and needed a break. He gently shooed his parents home and sent Tacy off for a long, hot shower. There would be time enough later to discuss Lois and her suspicious past.

"Were you a friend of my mom's too?"

Timmy's high voice interrupted his thoughts. He pulled his gaze toward his son, who was sitting up in bed, staring at him with big eyes.

"Steven said that he was friends with my mom when they were kids, so I wondered if you were friends too. Are you and Steven twins? My friend Matt is a twin, but he has a sister, not a brother. It would be cool to have a twin brother. Or just a brother."

That was a lot of information. There were a couple of questions packed with all that rambling. Which was he supposed to answer first? Timmy was looking at him expectantly, so he assumed some sort of response was required. He rubbed a hand across his jaw, feeling the beginnings of his five o'clock stubble.

"Uh, yeah," he finally said. "I mean, yeah, Steven and I are twins. And yeah, it's nice to have a brother. Sometimes. Oh, and yeah, your mom and I were friends growing up."

Friends. That word brought a surge of emotion in his chest. It was true. They had been friends. Best friends. Long before he had started to date her, Tacy had trailed along behind him and Steven, worming her way into their hearts. At first, he and Steven had just tolerated her, reveling in the fact that she was a Tolbert, one of their forbidden enemies. But it hadn't taken long for her to win them over. Carefree and tough, she had been game for all of his and Steven's hijinks and pranks. And then her mom left, and Tacy changed. Hidden under a show of bravado and stubbornness, their once spunky sidekick became fragile and lost. He couldn't have been much older than Timmy was now when he had realized that he wanted to do everything in his power to make her happy again. And that had set the tone for their relationship. He became her champion, her confidant, her best friend.

"If I had a brother, I think that I would want an older brother so that he could teach me stuff. I really want to try pitching, but I don't know how to do the wind-up. A brother could show me how."

Seb took a deep breath. Now wasn't the time to dwell on thoughts about how Timmy might've had had a sibling if Tacy hadn't filed for divorce. Or better yet, he'd have had a *dad* to teach him things. "Well, if you want to learn about baseball then you're staying in the right house, because both Steven and I played ball in high school. Steven even pitched some. He had a mean fastball and solid change-up. So, if you stick around here, we could teach you a few tricks."

Timmy's eyes shone as he beamed up at him. "That would be awesome."

Seb smiled back down at the boy, swallowing the lump in his throat. It was amazing that he could make the kid so happy with just the simple offer to toss around a baseball. He racked his brain for other possible conversation topics. "So, uh, do you root for the Rockies?"

"Yeah, but I've only ever been to one game. Grandpa took me. It was pretty cool. There were fireworks and a jet flew over the stadium. And Grandpa and I even got on the Megatron during the seventh inning stretch."

Seb flinched. It hurt to hear Timmy refer to Keith Tolbert as "Grandpa" when his own parents were stuck being called by their first names and treated as strangers. But it wasn't hard to imagine that Tacy's fiercely protective father had been equally protective of her son. "Do they still sing *Take Me out to the Ball Game* during the seventh inning stretch?"

"Yep. Grandpa knew all the words and how to hold up your fingers at the end."

He raised an eyebrow. Now that would be a sight to see. Keith Tolbert in his neat, buttoned-down dress shirt, singing along at a ball game. Seb ambled across the room to the spot where his old guitar hung on the wall.

He picked up the instrument and walked back toward Timmy, his fingers plucking the strings. It was out of tune, and he only knew a few chords. But he could strum out a simple song.

His son looked at him. The smile on Timmy's face and the trust in his eyes felt like a sucker punch in the gut. More than anything in the world, he wanted to be worthy of his son's admiration. In this whole mess of a situation—finding out that Tacy had kept such a crucial secret from him, and learning that Tacy and possibly Timmy, too, were in danger—the chance to get to know his son was a perfect, amazing gift. He wanted to bask in it and let everything else fall away, but that just wasn't an option. The danger was real, and it would be up to him to protect Tacy and Timmy from an adversary he didn't yet know and whose motives he couldn't understand.

He could only pray that he'd be enough to keep them safe.

Tacy pulled her long hair back and considered the fact that she and her son would be spending the night in the Hunts' bunkhouse. It was mind-boggling. As was the thought of Seb in the next room, chatting with Timmy.

She tucked her hairbrush into her kit and opened the bedroom door. She blinked, blinked again, and then closed her eyes.

She wasn't prepared for this. It wasn't fair.

It had been hard enough to see Seb again. But this was too much. Years of hearing him sing in the church choir should have dulled her appreciation for the low, rich resonance of his voice. But the last ten years had deepened his natural baritone and added layers of maturity. And what pulled even harder at her heart was the sound of Timmy joining in with the song. Her son's face was full of joy as he belted out the final words,

"'Cause it's one, two, three strikes you're out at the old ball game!"

She staggered backwards and bumped her arm against the wall. Two heads swiveled to face her.

"Hi, Mom. Seb and I were just talking about baseball. He and Steven are going to teach me how to pitch a fastball."

Wow. It had only taken one evening and Seb had already found the key to Timmy's heart. Baseball was a subject she knew little about. She tried, of course, for Timmy's sake—but she couldn't give him tips or help him practice. Seb could. And Timmy seemed so happy and comfortable, so how could she complain? She could feel Seb watching her, but she kept her eyes on Timmy.

"That's great. Seb probably didn't mention it, but he was the captain of his baseball team. However, right now it's way past your bedtime, so we better say prayers and shut off the lights." She sensed rather than saw Seb stand up and slip out the door as she knelt down beside Timmy's bed.

"Thank you, God, for this day," she prayed. "Thank you for old friends and sunshine and for your beautiful creation. Hold Timmy close in the palm of your hand. Bless him now and always, amen." *And please, Lord, keep all of us safe from the danger.*

Timmy's big eyes looked up at her. "And thank you also for Steven and Seb who are going to help me work on my pitching."

She pushed back tears and watched as he snuggled down in the blankets and closed his eyes. He was so trusting and so innocent. She leaned forward, pressed her lips against Timmy's forehead and watched the gentle rise and fall of his chest. No matter what, she had to protect him.

Bizzzzzup. Bizzzzzup.

What was that? The whirring sound was coming from the other side of the bunkhouse. She shut the door to Timmy's room and spotted Seb standing on the threshold, an electric screwdriver in his hand. His shirtsleeves were rolled up to reveal his tanned, muscular arms, and his dark eyes were narrowed with concentration.

Her heart did a soft flip in her chest as Seb looked over and saw her watching him. "Sorry for the noise," he whispered. "I borrowed the old lock from my parents' shed to add extra security to the door."

She pulled herself back to reality. The hit-and-run. The spider. Timmy, asleep in the next room. She needed to get a grip on her emotions. She couldn't afford to get caught up in nostalgia and forget the threat against her—and the risk to her son. She watched Seb affix another screw. His dark brown hair was longer than it had been in high school, and the lines around his eyes showed his age. But he still looked like the boy she had known ten years ago. The boy who had taught her how to canoe and fish. Who had protected her from the taunts of the mean girls who had laughed at her clothes. Who had asked her to marry him. A lump formed in her throat and she pushed back her tears. *What happened*? she wanted to ask him. *How could you leave me alone in the hospital?*

It was so difficult to be here with him. This was where he had kissed her for the first time. Not a romantic kiss, just a comforting peck on the top of her head. But what happened that day was forever burned into her mind. It was the day her mother left. She remembered her grandfather shouting, her father slamming the door, the squeal of a car driving away. She remembered tiptoeing down the hall and peeking into her grandfather's study and seeing her father sitting there with his head in his hands. She had slipped out of the house and run as fast as her legs could carry her to the one place she felt safe. The Hunts' bunkhouse.

That was where Seb had found her, sitting on the floor, knees pulled up under her chin, crying. He had walked in, put his arms around her and said, "Don't worry. Everything's going to be okay." Of course, everything was not okay. Her mother returned a week later to collect her stuff. Her father became closed off emotionally and overly protective. Her grandfather blamed her dad for losing interest in the ranch. And she was left with crushing guilt that she had somehow caused it all to happen, that had she been a different sort of kid, her mother might have stayed. But even though everything felt broken, Seb had been there for her—attending her piano recitals, cheering for her at track meets, taking her to the school dances. Of course, she had fallen in love with him, never dreaming that he would feel the same way about her.

But he did. At least he said that he did. She wondered if any of it was real.

And, now, she was here, back in the same place, and once again he was trying to protect her. The same warm, familiar feelings swelled her chest—but this time, she wasn't sure she could trust them, now or ever again.

Seb slid the lock back and forth a few times. "If it's okay with you, I'll bunk here on the couch." Her concern must have shown on her face because he was quick to add, "I'm still on board with keeping the truth from Timmy." She nodded, relieved. "He's a great kid, Tace. You did a good job, raising him on your own."

"My dad was with me all the way."

He grimaced. "Hey, uh, can we talk about something else for a moment?"

He stepped outside and waited for her to follow. She closed the door softly. The hairs on her arm prickled as Seb sat down beside her.

"I dug a bit more into Lois's background, and it isn't good."

Lois. Right. "What did you find out?"

"She's moved around a bit. Changed her name at least twice, and her last two husbands died under mysterious circumstances."

"What do you mean by 'mysterious circumstances'? Is my grandfather in danger? Should I call him?"

"I think you should wait until we have more information. If Steven or my mom can watch Timmy tomorrow morning, I'll drive you into town and you can meet with the sheriff. He can do some more digging into Lois while he investigates the attacks against you so far."

A shiver of fear ran down her spine as the reality of the situation hit her like a ton of bricks. One minute she felt protected and secure, the next, terrified. There was a target on her back, and there was no safe space. She was stuck, lying low in the Tolberts' bunkhouse, relying on her ex-husband, the man who still made her heart beat double-time in her chest.

SEVEN

The next morning, Tacy drove into town to see the sheriff. The interview went a lot better than she had expected.

It helped to have Seb along for moral support. The sheriff took notes and thumbed through the pictures Seb had taken when he returned to scene the day after the accident. He had snapped a couple of photos of her battered bike, and the sight of the bent frame and flattened tires sent a new flurry of tremors down her spine. If the angle of impact had been just a little different, she might well be dead. That certainly seemed to be the driver's intent.

The sheriff planned to notify local repair shops to be on the lookout for a vehicle with a dent in the front bumper. "Be careful, Ms. Tolbert," he said as he walked them to the door. "Someone seems determined to hurt you, and you need to stay on guard."

Seb reached over and squeezed her hand. It

was the same thing he had been saying since he rescued her from the buffalo stampede. She was doing her best to comply, but danger just kept finding her.

So, it was one difficult task down, and one to go. As soon as she and Seb returned to the ranch, she began to prepare to meet with her grandfather. She couldn't delay any longer in telling him about Timmy. But it wasn't going to be easy to explain the rationale for her deception. He had been so angry when he learned that she had moved in with the Hunts. How would he react when she told him about his great grandson?

She arrived at the ranch house early, and Lois, still in her dressing gown, led her into the dining room to wait. Tacy's eyes were drawn to the table set for four. Lois followed her glance and was quick to explain.

"I hope you don't mind, dear. Carl invited Gunnar Graff to join us for dinner."

Mixed emotions filled her. It would be lovely to see her godfather—her father's best friend. But his presence here tonight meant that her big revelation would have to wait.

She took advantage of her time alone to enjoy the view of the sandstone hills that rose up along the border of the ranch. It was just a sliver of the four-thousand-acre spread that had been in the Tolbert family for over a hundred years, but it represented everything she had loved about growing up in North Dakota. She could have stood there all night if it hadn't been for the trill of the doorbell, announcing the arrival of their guest.

The sound of voices drifted into the dining room, Lois and Carl welcoming Gunnar with hugs and easy banter. Tacy peeked into the foyer. Lois's long, dark hair was pinned off her neck in an elaborate chignon, and her grandfather's arm was wrapped around her waist. Gunnar turned and spotted her. He stepped into the room and pulled her into a tight embrace.

"It's good to see you, Tacy girl." Even after ten years, that gravelly voice was distinctively familiar. And though his wavy hair was grayer than she remembered, he still radiated his own particular brand of confidence and charm.

"You, too, Gunnar," she said, taking in the familiar scent of Old Spice aftershave and peppermint. "I'm glad for the chance to tell you in person how much your calls and emails meant to my dad all the way up to the end."

"Nonsense. Your father's friendship was a gift to me."

"Hello, Tacy." Her grandfather elbowed past them on his way toward the table.

"Hi, Grandfather. Thank you for inviting me here today."

Gunnar hung back and took her arm. He lowered his voice to a whisper. "I wanted to tell you that I was sorry I didn't make it in for the funeral. But Keith and I had a good talk before he passed. He told me he had written to Carl, and I was glad. The two of them should never have fallen out the way they did. Maybe his letter will help your grandfather understand his reasons for leaving. And my offer to help still stands. If I can assist with the estate or with probate, just give a call."

"I might take you up on that somewhere down the line. I brought along some of my dad's papers to give to my grandfather. But he didn't own any property, so I ought to be able to handle the estate."

"Of course. I sometimes forget that you're almost officially a lawyer yourself now. I hope you'll let me know when you pass the bar so that I can pass along my congratulations. One of the last things your dad said to me was how he was proud of all of your accomplishments."

"Thanks, Gunnar." Her voice broke, and she bit down on her lip to keep from crying. Gunnar didn't know about Timmy, but there was very little else that her dad hadn't shared during his frequent chats with his best friend. Talking to him was almost like talking to her father again.

She joined the others at the table. Once she was seated, her grandfather said grace.

"Father God. Thank you for this food and for bringing Tacy home to us and for giving us this time together. Amen."

Short and sweet. Her grandfather had never been much for long prayers, but the kindness of his words touched her heart.

Lois handed her a large basket of warm bread. "I'm glad that you've recovered so quickly from your injuries, though I wish you hadn't run off to the Hunts'. Of course, it was your choice, dear, even if it was…quite a surprise."

Gunnar's eyebrows shot up. "You're staying at the Hunts'?"

"I am," she said.

"Why?" Gunnar said.

Tacy took a long breath. How much to share? Some explanation was needed to justify her change in location, but she didn't want to raise more questions. "It's a long story. Even though our families were enemies because of the feud, Steven and Seb and I have always been friends."

A shadow of irritation crossed Gunnar's face. "Just remember that you need to be careful around the Hunts. They've always been trying to get their hands on Tolbert land. No doubt, they're angry that Carl rejected their son's offer to buy the ranch."

Her grandfather blew out a frustrated sigh. "This whole thing has gotten so complicated that I'm starting to think I need to consider other options. I know I've signed a purchase agreement, but at this point, nothing's set in stone. Maybe I could lease the property while Lois and I head out to see the world."

"We haven't closed the door on anything yet," Gunnar agreed. "But you claimed you wanted to make a clean break. Leasing will just delay the inevitable. The long-term decision would always be hanging over your head."

After that, they let the subject drop. The rest of the meal passed without any further mention of the ranch or the impending sale.

"Dessert, anyone?" Lois asked. "I ordered us a delicious treat from the Whirlybird Bakery."

"That sounds great," Tacy said as the glare of headlights lit up the dining room window.

"Are you expecting other guests?" Gunnar asked.

"No." Lois lifted her arm to shield her eyes from the brilliance of the lights.

Tacy moved toward the window. Her breath hitched as a familiar green F-150 pulled to a stop in front of the house. A minute later, Seb and Steven stepped out of the cab and headed toward the front door.

Now what were they doing here? And how would her grandfather react to having his fortress invaded by the Hunts?

"I'm beginning to think that this was a really bad idea," Steven said.

Seb shook his head. "We can't leave now. Besides, you know what Mom will say if we bring back her pie. Though I guess we could eat it ourselves and hope she doesn't ask questions. Besides, we're doing this to support Tacy."

At least that was the plan. He had his doubts about whether or not Tacy would appreciate the gesture. She had been so worried about the visit to her grandfather that it seemed like a good idea to show up and help her explain about Timmy. Maybe Carl Tolbert wouldn't be so angry if he knew that they had all been in the same boat. At least that had been his motivation when he came up with the idea. And when his mom handed him the pie and offered to watch Timmy, it was just a matter of enlisting Steven as his wing man to crash the event.

But now that he and Steven were actually standing on the front stoop, a wave of uneasiness swept through his veins. Were they making a mistake? This was Tolbert property. Even in all their time hanging out with Tacy when they were growing up, he and Steven had not crossed over further than the disputed never-never land. More than once, Carl had threatened his father about setting foot on his acreage. There was no way that he and Steven would be welcome here.

There was a click of a latch being turned from the inside. The door swung open to reveal a wide, carpeted staircase and a long hall. Backlit by the lamp on the console stood Carl Tolbert, looking much the same as he had when they met at the hospital. The same grizzled countenance. The same canny intelligence radiating from those piercing blue eyes. All that was missing was his trademark tan cowboy hat, and Seb could see that hanging on the hook by the door.

The old man glared as he blocked their entry. "Steven. Sebastian. To what do I owe this unexpected visit?"

"My mom thought you might enjoy an apple pie." Seb handed the dish to Carl, who set it down on the sideboard.

"Thank you," he said. He seemed mollified by their goodwill offering. "This is my wife, Lois Tolbert."

"It's nice to meet you, ma'am." Seb forced himself to return her smile.

"We were just about to have some dessert. Would you care to join us?" she asked.

"We'd like that," Seb said. He was grateful for Lois's graciousness since Carl certainly seemed disinclined to invite them in.

They turned and followed Lois into the dining room where Gunnar Graff occupied a seat in the middle of the table, directly next to Tacy. Well, that was unfortunate. Seb suppressed a groan. The Tolberts' attorney had always been one of his least favorite people in Chimney Bluff, as he shared the Tolberts' grudge against the Hunts.

As soon as they were seated, Carl cleared his throat and turned his head in Seb's direction.

"Now that things have settled down, I suppose I should thank you for accompanying my granddaughter to the hospital and for keeping her company until I could arrive. I heard that you also helped her avoid that bison herd of yours after one of your ranch hands forgot to secure the gate."

Seb bit back a sharp retort. Maybe that was true, maybe not—but it was typical of Carl to assume the Hunts bore the blame. Seb looked at Tacy, whose fixed expression was impossible to read.

Carl continued. "And I'm glad you got a chance to meet my wife. Hard to believe such a beautiful woman would agree to marry an old antique like me. But she did, and I thank God every day for sending her into my life."

Lois patted Carl's hand to acknowledge the compliment, but there was a flicker of sadness behind her eyes. "I think it's lovely to have neighbors stop by to visit. And I want you to know that I don't put much stock in any of this talk of a long-standing feud. I'm delighted by the opportunity to break bread with our neighbors. And to that end, we have chocolate cake, and thanks to your mother, homemade pie. So, there's plenty for everyone. Excuse me while I get the other dessert and a couple extra plates."

"I'll help you," Gunnar said.

Seb turned his head to watch them walk toward the kitchen. Lois sure wasn't what he had expected. It was hard to imagine her plotting against Tacy. But his MP training had taught him that looks were often deceiving.

They returned a few minutes later, Lois with a white cardboard box with a sticker on top, proclaiming that the product was peanut-free, and Gunnar with the pie and the extra plates.

"Cake? Or pie?" Lois's bejeweled fingers fluttered in the air. "Or perhaps a small sliver of both."

"How about a big piece of both?" Carl said.

As Lois bent to cut the cake, the sparkle of a large diamond on her left hand caught the light.

That was some rock on Lois's finger. As Seb turned to accept a slice of chocolate cake, a pang of guilt shot through his senses. He remembered the tiny ring he had bought Tacy at the PX. It had cost three hundred dollars, which, at the time had seemed like a fortune.

Lois settled back on the carved oak chair next to Carl at the table. "This room is one of my favorites at the ranch. When I was helping prepare the listing, I made sure to include reference to the hand-hewn floor and the beautiful bay window."

"About the listing," Steven said. "This might not be the right time to talk business, but I heard you had an offer from an outside buyer. It would be a disaster if the place was bought up by one of those huge conglomerates that swoop in and strip all the resources from the land."

Carl Tolbert's eyes flashed with irritation. "Despite what you may think, young man, I'm aware that there are plenty of people out there who aren't good stewards of the land, and I'm not such a fool as to miss reading the fine print. I've worked this place for over fifty years, and I know my responsibility to the community. I've been fair in dealing with everyone who crossed my path. As for the sale, nothing is settled at this point. The mineral surveys and assessments were just wrapped up this week, so there's still lots to do before the deal is final."

Clang!

Tacy's fork dropped against her plate. Her mouth fell open, gasping for air.

Oh, no. Seb's eyes went to the half-eaten slivers of cake and pie on her plate. Tacy was having an allergic reaction. There must have been peanut products in the dessert. "She's in anaphylactic shock. Tacy? Tacy? Where is your EpiPen?"

She couldn't answer. Her head was rolled back, and her body had already started to slide forward, out of the chair.

He grasped her waist and he lowered her to the floor. "Somebody call 911. I'll find her EpiPen. Where's her purse?"

"It's in the hall." Carl said.

"I'll call the paramedics," Steven said.

Seb rushed toward the entryway, his eyes zeroing in on the hooks along the wall. There it was. A small red leather purse, with a set of keys dangling from the strap. He flipped it over, and a wallet and a pair of sunglasses thumped onto the floor. No EpiPen. "Maybe she left it at the bunkhouse."

But driving back there would take too long. Wait. What was that? A familiar backpack had been set next to a pair of Carl's boots on the floor. Tacy must have forgotten it when she rushed off to meet Steven the day after the accident. He unzipped the top flap and dug inside. Seconds later, his fingers locked on the cylindrical shape of an EpiPen.

"Got it," he said, spinning around and heading back into the dining room.

"I'm going to turn on the outside light and wait out front for the ambulance." Gunnar's voice boomed from behind him.

"Good idea." Seb rolled up the hem of Tacy's skirt and placed the orange tip of the pen on her right thigh. He pushed, and—*click*.

He held the needle in place for five seconds and then pulled it free. Then he massaged the site of the injection.

In the background, he could hear Steven giving the 911 operator an update on the situation. "My brother just gave her the injection." Steven held the phone away from his mouth. "The ambulance is still a few minutes out. They want to know if she's conscious."

Tacy groaned and opened her eyes. "What?" she said.

"You're okay, Tace. Just hang in there." He looked up at Steven. "Tell them that the medicine seems to be working."

Tacy forced a wobbly smile. "I'm good. I feel fine."

"Glad to hear it. But the paramedics are still going to want to check you out." And besides, the sooner Tacy was away from her Grandfather's ranch the better. There was no way that this was an accident. His mom had taken pains to ensure that her pie was peanut-free, which meant something else at the dinner must have caused the allergic reaction.

The high-pitched whir of a siren cut through the air.

Carl stepped forward, his brow knitted with worry and anger. "I'm going with Tacy to the hospital. I just don't understand how something like this could have happened in my own house. It must have been the pie. I should have known not to trust Hunts bearing gifts."

EIGHT

The hands on the clock were nudging close to midnight when Tacy climbed into her grandfather's truck for the ride home from the hospital. If she looked rough after four hours spent in the emergency room, he looked even worse for the wear. Dark circles rimmed the bottoms of his tired eyes, and his mouth was bent in an anxious frown.

"Thank you for staying with me at the hospital," she said.

"My pleasure," he said. "How are you feeling now?"

"Much better than I did a couple hours ago, that's for sure."

"What did that intern say before he signed your release? I should have taken notes when he was issuing his orders."

"Are you kidding? You were a rock star, asking questions and making sure I was good to go. I had the easy part. I got to stretch out on the bed while you sat in that uncomfortable plastic chair."

"You were very brave. I was proud of you. But I'd feel a lot better if I could bring you home with me instead of dropping you off at the Hunts'."

Tacy swallowed hard. There were so many things she wanted to share. But he looked so tired and frail. And definitely too exhausted to hear about Timmy. But she'd have to tell him sooner rather than later, before he heard the news from someone else.

As they pulled in front of the bunkhouse, she turned to face him with a weary smile. "What do you say that we both tuck in and get some sleep. Maybe we can meet at Dot's later today and really talk."

Her grandfather nodded. "I'd like that, but not today. This afternoon, I have an appointment in Bismarck with my heart doctor. Nothing serious. Just a routine check."

Heart doctor? Was he really okay? Obviously, it was the right decision to postpone her big revelation. "I hope you can get some sleep before setting off on the drive."

"I'll be able to rest until ten. But Lois won't have that luxury. She'll open her flower shop and then stop back at noon to go with me, so I won't have to make the drive alone."

"I'm glad you'll have company. Is it hard for Lois to take time away from the store?"

"Not right now." Her grandfather's lips formed a half smile. "The flower shop is more of a hobby. But she's also working on verifying her real estate credentials, so she's keeping busy."

"Does that mean Lois is handling the sale of the ranch?"

"With Gunnar's help, of course. We thought it would save time and some of the fees if she was involved. She did a lot of work with real estate in Reno, so she's had some experience with this sort of thing. You know me. I'm a rancher, not a businessman. I'm glad to let the experts take the lead on this. When and if a decision is made, I'll be there to sign on the dotted line."

"I get it," Tacy said. But she had some doubts that such a lackadaisical approach was the right way to proceed with such an important transaction. Especially since she had a few doubts about Lois, herself. "I'd be happy to look at the documents if you need another opinion."

"That shouldn't be necessary. Lois and Gunnar have the situation well in hand. You know, I've made no secret that I'd rather not leave Chimney Bluff. But it will make Lois happy, and that's important to me."

"She's your wife. You need to do what is best for your marriage."

"A lot of people probably think that it was an impulsive decision for me to marry again after all these years. But as soon as I saw Lois, I knew I wouldn't rest until she agreed to be my wife. She's beautiful, of course. But what attracted me most was her vulnerability. She's like a tender blossom, clinging to the vine."

She smiled, and Carl shook his head. "I know. It sounds like a cliché, but it's true. She puts on a good face, but life has dealt her some serious blows. She lost her husband and all her possessions in a devastating house fire. She barely escaped with her life."

"How awful." But hadn't Seb said that the fire was being investigated as arson? And what about her first husband, who also died under mysterious circumstances?

"Awful doesn't even begin to describe it. I thought it would be a tonic to bring her home to the ranch. I always believed that this place was created by God to calm the troubled soul."

God's country. That was exactly what her father always said.

She thought back to the last moments she and her father had spent in Chimney Bluff, ten years earlier. Before that day, she had never seen her father cry, not even when her mother walked out on them. But he had broken down that morning when they crossed the state line. She remembered it as vividly as if it had been yesterday. Her tall, handsome father, clutching the steering wheel in a white-knuckled grip as tears ran down his face.

She took a deep breath as overwhelming grief threatened to squeeze all the air from her chest. *Oh, Dad. How badly were you hurting that you could never come back, not even for a visit?*

Her grandfather shifted his eyes away from the road. "I told Lois that your showing up like this is a sign that the rush to put the ranch on the market is a big mistake. Not that you'd want to live here again. But if you did, I hope you'd feel comfortable enough to tell me, so I could stop the sale before it was too late."

Her eyes filled with fresh tears.

"Don't cry, darlin'. I'm sorry for putting you on the spot, especially when you're still recovering from what happened at dinner. You almost died right there in the dining room, with all of us watching, unable to help."

"You *did* help. And Seb was an MP in the military, so he knew how to give an injection."

"I'd still like to identify the culprit here. The bakery or the Hunts? Actually, it would be easy to find out. There's a half of pie left, and we can have it analyzed. And the lawyers can handle the rest."

Lawyers? Please, no. Was this crazy feud ever going to end? Future generations will probably find it hard to believe that the two families almost come to blows over peanut products in a cake.

Or a pie.

Not that she suspected the Hunts for even a moment. But then, what had happened? Could Lois really have deliberately added peanuts to the cake? The drum of her heartbeat quickened its pace, and her throat tightened as she recalled her allergic reaction. One minute, she had been sitting at the table, eating dessert, the next she hadn't been able to breathe.

Cold realization washed over her. If Seb hadn't been there last night, she might have died. But why would Lois want to kill her? Seb's theory—that the motive revolved around the sale of the ranch—offered as many questions as answers. And would her grandfather ever believe that his new wife wanted his granddaughter dead?

Seb was exhausted. A few hours earlier, he had returned to the bunkhouse to relieve his parents, who had been watching Timmy. But he couldn't sleep. Every time he closed his eyes, he was back in the Tolberts' dining room, watching helplessly as Tacy went into anaphylactic shock. No matter how hard he tried, he couldn't banish the image of her terrified face or stop the sound of Carl Tolbert's angry voice from playing in his head.

I should have known not to trust a Hunt bearing gifts.

It had taken all his will power to ignore the accusation and keep the focus on Tacy, where it belonged.

But now, with Timmy tucked safely in bed, he had plenty of time to think. And the longer he considered the facts, the more he was convinced that what happened that evening was yet another deliberate attack against Tacy.

But who had tampered with the dessert? He knew who he suspected, but he couldn't let himself jump to conclusions. That was no way to run an investigation.

He eliminated Carl from consideration. And, as much as he didn't like or trust the Tolberts' attorney, he couldn't come up with a motive to pin on Gunnar that would justify murder.

Which left Lois. She had ample time to tamper with the cake, just as she had the means to put something in Tacy's coffee the day of the stampede. Too bad the doctor's office still hadn't returned the results of the drug test.

But apart from all of the circumstantial evidence, he still needed to come up with a concrete reason to explain why Lois would want to kill Tacy.

A car door slammed.

He walked over to the window. The porch light was on, and he could see Tacy lean over and kiss her grandfather's cheek. A second later, her footsteps sounded on the steps, followed by the *vroom* of a motor as Carl pulled away.

Tacy paused and reached into her purse. Was she looking for her keys? He hurried across the room and opened the door.

Tacy smiled as she stepped toward him. "Hey! What are you doing still awake?"

"I…" His answer hung in the cool night air as the crunch and snap of something moving in the nearby bushes sent his senses into high alert. His brain registered the possible threat as his body reacted on instinct. He leapt forward, covering the remaining two feet between him and Tacy, his eyes frantically scanning the shadows.

Positioning his body in front of Tacy, he pulled her across the threshold and into the bunkhouse and then slammed the door behind them. As the latch clicked, he reached for the deadbolt and slid it into the grove.

"Seb?" Tacy stammered. "What's happening?"

He shook his head. His body felt like a chord

being pulled too tight, but he didn't want to cause unnecessary worry. He took a steadying breath.

"I'm not sure. I heard a branch crack near the porch. It might have been a raccoon or a fox trampling around in the undergrowth, but it seemed best to get inside as quickly as possible."

He walked toward the main window and peered through. Was that a bit of movement near the bushes? More likely it was a rodent or some other small vermin, but he couldn't shake his anxiety drumming in his brain.

Tacy didn't seem to pick up on his unease as she made a beeline for Timmy's bedroom. She peaked inside and then closed the door. "He's sound asleep," she said. But her smile was replaced by a look of alarm as she pointed to his right arm. "You must have caught your hand on that loose nail on the door."

He glanced down, surprised to see the red trickle of blood and feel the faint sting of pain. He hadn't even realized that he had cut himself. "It's just a scratch."

"Maybe. But it can't hurt to treat it with antiseptic. Where's the first aid kit?"

"In the bathroom medicine cabinet under the sink."

"Okay. I'll be right back." She headed across the room, returning a minute later with a small white box with a red cross on the top. She sat down next to him, squirted a dollop of antibacterial cream onto the cut and massaged it in with her fingers.

Her eyes were soft as she looked at him and smiled. "I've gotten to be quite an expert at this stuff. When Timmy was seven, he wanted to be a ninja warrior. After a few dozen cuts and bruises, he learned his lesson and became more careful."

Seb grinned. Sounded like a chip off the old block, though the whole thing must have been a trial for Tacy. He kept his arm still as Tacy completed her ministrations. How had he forgotten the cute way she squinted when she concentrated, or how the touch of her fingers had always sent shockwaves across his heart?

"Seb?" she said. "I didn't know that Steven was trying to buy my grandfather's ranch."

"Yeah. He and a bunch of his buddies have been looking for land they could use as a sanctuary for bulls too old or injured to ride. He's all in on the project, and that property would have been perfect, so he was disappointed that his bid wasn't given proper consideration."

"I'm sorry to hear that." She tilted her head, her eyes roaming across his face as she tightened the bandage in place. "Does that feel okay?"

"Umm…yeah." She probably didn't want to hear about the avalanche of memories tumbling across his brain.

He waited a minute, and then he walked across the room and sat down on the ottoman.

New subject. Safe subject. Timmy.

"So, our boy was completely sacked out when I got back to the bunkhouse. My mom said he nodded off early. She taught him cribbage. I think she let him win."

"She's been so lovely." Tacy sank down onto the couch and forced a wobbly smile.

"How about you? What happened at the hospital?"

"They kept me for a few hours under observation since I had such a severe reaction."

"I know I'm starting to sound like a broken record, but I think one or both of the desserts were laced with some type of peanut product."

"It's a good thing that I always carry an EpiPen in my purse."

"Uh, Tace. There was nothing in your purse. The one I found was in your backpack."

She shook her head. "That doesn't make sense. I specifically remember tucking one next to my wallet before I left to drive to the ranch."

He blew out a long breath. It appeared that whoever had tampered with the desserts had also removed Tacy's EpiPen from her purse.

"Lois?"

"She's the logical suspect. We can talk more about this in the morning when we're rested and awake."

"Good call." Tacy pushed back her shoulders and straightened her neck. "The exhaustion seems to be finally catching up to me. I suppose it's time to head off to bed."

He nodded. "You should sleep in tomorrow. I'll get up early and make Timmy breakfast. It's time I start figuring out how to be a regular dad."

But for the moment at least, he would remain in the role of defender and protector. He waited a few minutes until he was sure Tacy was in bed. Then, he crept out onto the porch and set off on a brisk stroll around the premises. He couldn't quite shake the suspicion that the snap of the branch he'd heard earlier hadn't been an animal but someone lurking nearby. With the beam of his flashlight trained to the ground, he scanned the area for signs of an intruder.

The soil was too dry for any tracks, but there were several broken branches smashed against the dirt. He paused. A small rodent wouldn't be heavy enough to cause such damage. He took a step closer to make a better assessment. The bushes crackled. He jumped backwards as a large badger scuttled toward him.

Was this the midnight prowler? Or had there been something—or someone—else lurking around the bunkhouse, hiding in the shadows of the night?

NINE

Functioning effectively on less than five hours of sleep was proving to be a challenge. Coffee helped. Seb had just put on a fresh pot when Timmy joined him in the kitchen.

"Why is Mom still sleeping?" he said. "She's always awake before me. When Sandy tucked me in last night, she promised I'd see Mom first thing in the morning."

"Your mom had a rough night, so she going to sleep in today a little longer than usual. What do you say you get dressed while I rustle up some breakfast, and then maybe we can find a bat and ball and a couple of gloves in the shed?"

"Awesome," Timmy said.

Half an hour later, they were outside in front of the bunkhouse, tossing around a baseball.

Timmy had skills, he'd give him that. He handled pop flies and grounders and tossed the ball back with the flick of his wrist.

"You play first base, right?"

"Usually." Timmy nodded. "But sometimes the coach puts me in the outfield. We have games twice a week. They're at night, so my mom can come and watch me play."

Seb shook his head. How did Tacy do it? Working full-time, caring for her dad, and attending law school, yet she still managed to make it to all those baseball games. A sudden realization nudged his brain. This would be his life when Timmy came to visit. Grabbing breakfast-on-the-run and standing on the sidelines at baseball games. Not to mention dealing with the responsibilities of school and homework. The choice between moving to DC or staying in Chimney Bluff suddenly seemed a lot more complicated than he had imagined.

As Seb tossed the fly ball back to Timmy, Steven appeared, a canvas sack of old bats slung over his shoulder. "I thought we could try to have a real game."

Five minutes later, they were ready to play. Seb batted first. Steven struck him out on four pitches with a wicked fastball. That was embarrassing. Then Timmy took his turn in the batter's box.

"Wait a sec." Seb reached into his back pocket and snapped a quick picture of the nine-year-old slugger at the plate. He was putting his phone away when Timmy hit a hard drive to the out-field.

Timmy's legs pumped furiously as he rounded first and headed for second. Steven chased the ball and attempted a tag at third, but Timmy streamed by him, determined to score.

"Safe!" Seb shouted as Timmy slid into home.

Timmy brushed himself off and beamed. Seb tousled his son's hair and then tossed his glove down onto the grass. "You guys keep playing," he called out as he headed toward the bunk-house. "I'm going to head inside to check on Tacy. If she's awake, I'll see if she wants to join us, just in case Timmy hits another awesome home run."

Click. Swish.

What was that? Metal scraping against wood? Tacy tensed as her eyes popped open.

"Hello?" She braved a glance around the room. The shades were closed, and a narrow band of light outlined the windows' wide perimeter. She reached across the nightstand for her phone and powered on the flashlight. "Who's there?" Her fingers shook as she pointed the thin beam toward the door and then the window. Nothing.

A sigh of relief escaped from her lips. The noise she had heard was probably Timmy in the front room. She supposed she ought to get up and see what he needed, but she wasn't ready to get up quite yet. She set her phone next to her pillow and stretched out on her back. She sank back into a delicious wave of exhaustion, closed her eyes, and…

Creeeeak.

The footsteps she heard definitely weren't in the front room—they were in her room. And those weren't Timmy's steps.

A pulse of fear pumped through her veins. She pressed her eyes closed and listened.

Another creak, followed by the slam of a drawer and the crash of something falling to the floor.

She pulled the covers over her head, and slowly edged her hand toward the pillow, fumbling for her phone. But before her fingers could close on the case, something soft and plush slammed down on her face.

Her breaths came fast and furious as she flailed against the hands pushing the pillow over her mouth. She arched her back and struggled to grasp hold of her assailant's wrist. But no matter how she tried, she couldn't dislodge the force pressing harder and harder until there was no air left in her lungs at all.

Help me, Lord. Her chest heaved against the blackness.

A door slammed in the living room.

The hands pressing against her face held fast for another second and then released. She gagged in a mouthful of air as her fingers tried to tear the suffocating pillow free, but her oxygen-deprived body felt sluggish and unresponsive. Footsteps shuffled against the floorboards beside her bed. Her assailant seemed to be on the move.

More air leaked in around the edges of the cotton case, and she gulped it in furiously. She was finally able to reach around and push the pillow onto the floor. Free at last, she lay flat on her back, gasping for breath. A shadow passed in front the window, followed by a clatter and thump. Was her assailant escaping? She wanted to shake off the malaise that was dragging at her senses, but she was too weak.

"Tacy?" Seb's voice sounded muffled and far away.

"I'm here." Her legs felt like jelly as she skidded across the room. Her fingers turned the lock on her bedroom door. It snapped open, and she flicked on the light.

Seb stood in the doorway. "I heard a thump. What happened?"

Tears clouded her vision. "Someone tried to suffocate me. But when you came into the bunkhouse, he ran away."

Steven appeared behind Seb on the threshold. "It's crazy that someone broke in here in the middle of the day. Don't worry about Timmy, Tace. He's in the living room with my dad. He wanted to come in and wake you, but I guess it's a good thing he didn't. I'll tell them to go to the main house and wait for us there," Steven said, backing away. "Meanwhile, I'll circle around outside and see if I can find any signs of the intruder."

Tacy swayed sideways. All of a sudden, it felt as if her legs might collapse under her. Seb threaded an arm around her waist and led her over to a chair by the bed.

She sank down against the tattered cushion. "I thought I was going to die, Seb. I couldn't breathe, and he kept pushing down on the pillow."

"He?" Seb homed in on her description. "It was a man?"

Was it? All of a sudden, she wasn't sure. "I don't know." She shook her head. But why had she used a masculine pronoun? Her gaze swept past the upended suitcase, toward the papers and clothing tossed on the floor. What had the intruder been looking for in the dark? "I'm just grateful that Timmy wasn't here when it happened."

"Breathe, Tacy, breathe. Timmy's fine. You're

the one in danger. Look at this place. Whoever did this was searching for something, and you got in the way."

"How do I know if they found what they were looking for? Everything is such a mess."

"I'll help you do an inventory of your stuff later. After you talk to the sheriff."

The sheriff. Again. These endless attacks seemed to be a routine. Would she ever be safe? She reached for a sweatshirt that lay crumpled on the floor and pulled it over her head. That felt better. Warmer. More secure. She hugged her arms tightly around her waist.

Seb walked over to the window and looked at the jamb. "I should've checked the windows when I put the dead bolt on the front door. This is on me."

"No, it isn't. Nothing that has happened to me is your fault." Her fingers dug deeper into the sleeves of her sweatshirt. The memory of the pillow being smashed against her face produced a batch of fresh tears. She was angry and upset and tired of being afraid. She unclenched her arms, reached up and pushed back her tears. "But this isn't going to stop until we identify the person wants me dead."

He scrubbed his hand against his chin. "I'm grasping at straws here, but I keep coming back to the two variables that seem to have kick-started this whole mess—your arrival in town and your grandfather's decision to sell the ranch. And if we're going to home in on a motive, we need more information. Maybe the sale documents could provide some fresh clues."

A spark of exhilaration lit up her brain, and the possibility of finally doing something proactive fueled her enthusiasm. "Gunnar probably has the originals locked up in his safe. But my grandfather might have copies in his files at the ranch. And he and Lois will be in Bismarck for most of the afternoon. This could be the perfect opportunity to take a look."

"Not today, Tace," he said. "Not after everything you've been through."

She drummed her fingers against the chair, eagerness already coiling in her gut. Seb might be inclined to exercise caution, but it was her life that was being threatened. She glanced at her purse and thought about the key tucked in the side pocket that fit the lock on her grandfather's front door.

It was time to get some answers.

TEN

The sheriff arrived at the bunkhouse shortly before eleven with a couple of deputies who took pictures and dusted for prints. Tacy answered all his questions about the incident and promised to check her belongings to see if anything was missing. Her heart pounded as she described the attack and relived the terror of her near-suffocation.

Once the team packed up and returned to the station, Tacy and Seb climbed into his truck and headed for her grandfather's ranch. Even though the authorities were handling the case, she had not wavered in her resolve to search for the documents. Seb had tried to persuade her to wait, but her determination to act with or without him finally won him over to her plan. Timmy was going to stay at the main house with Sandy for the remainder of the afternoon, which would give her plenty of time to look through her grandfather's files.

The attack at the bunkhouse had clarified her thoughts. The only way to protect herself and her son would be for her to take an active role in identifying her attacker and putting the person behind bars. For the first time in a long time, she knew her own mind and trusted her judgment.

"Just promise that you'll be careful when you're inside," Seb said. "If you see anyone, make an excuse and get out immediately."

The plan was simple. She'd use her key to unlock the front door and make her way to her grandfather's office. Seb would wait in the truck on the side of the main road, about fifty yards from the curve. From there, he could see anyone turning down the driveway.

It wouldn't take long since she knew where to look. She'd be in and out in minutes. Easy peasy.

She hoped.

Inside the house, the brass knob of the office turned easily in her hand. She let out a long breath as she stepped across the threshold. Wow. Being in this room brought back a lot of memories. She and her father would stretch out on the large leather couch and read books while her grandfather balanced the accounts for the ranch. When he finished his paperwork, they would pull out the checkerboard and take turns playing against each other. She had forgotten how, despite their differences, they had always made it a point to spend time as a family.

Flicking on the overhead light, she padded over to the desk. If she remembered correctly, her grandfather stored most of his important papers in the cabinet below the credenza. She slid open the top drawer. Office supplies. She tried the second drawer and a smile twitched on her lips. *Bingo*. Hanging files with descriptions printed on the top—Taxes, Car Info, Health Insurance, Life Insurance. Her hand froze on the next file.

What was that? Her phone vibrated in her pocket.

A text from Seb. Lois is headed down the driveway.

How was that even possible?

Her insides clenched. Logic said she should leave...but she couldn't bear the thought of forfeiting the chance to find answers. Her eyes flicked around the office. There was a good chance that Lois might not even realize she was here. Especially if she turned off the overhead light. She scampered across the room and hit the switch. The open slats of the blinds provided enough illumination for her to finish her search.

She tiptoed back toward the credenza and knelt down beside the desk. Her fingers flipped over the labeled files. Where was the purchase offer? Finally, she found a folder within a folder entitled Conveyance. This had to be it. Inside were copies of the deeds to the property, beginning all the way back with Isaiah Tolbert, the first of the family to settle in Chimney Bluff. And yes—at the very bottom of the stack—was a purchase agreement, dated July of this year.

Her phone vibrated with yet another text. I'm following behind her on foot. She's at the front door.

The creak of the hinges from the front entrance stilled her hand. But only for a moment. She was about to close the file when something caught her eye—a copy of a quit claim deed. Was that her father's name on the document? She picked up the paper, her eyes darting across the legalese—"Carl Tolbert, grantor, hereby conveys to Carl Tolbert and Keith Tolbert, grantees, as tenants in common, property listed in Exhibit A." She flipped the page over. Sure enough, Exhibit A was the legal description of the ranch. Her mind raced to remember what she had learned in Property class in law school. She snatched up the pile and thrust it into her backpack, shoved the file drawer closed, pushed up on her knees and waited.

Heels clicked against the tile floor. Lois. She could make out her shadow, outlined by the light in the hall. Lois seemed to be moving past the door when Tacy's foot jerked and bumped the bottom of the credenza.

Whoosh.

The drawer slid out from the cabinet.

The footsteps stopped. Tacy's eyes darted toward the doorway. Uh-oh. Lois was paused on the threshold.

Tacy froze in place, hardly daring to breathe. Maybe if she stayed still, Lois would turn and leave.

But no. There was a click, and the room was bathed in a golden glow.

"Tacy?" Lois stood next to the light switch. "What are you doing in here in the dark?"

"I—I—" She struggled to answer.

Lois moved with surprising quickness across the room, clutching something long and sharp in her right hand. "Good grief, child. Did you walk all the way over from the bunkhouse? With your hurt leg?" She tucked the object she was holding behind her back. "You can't be fully recovered yet after last night's ordeal."

"I'm fine. I stopped by to get something I left here in all the rush, and I…um…was passing by the study. And I…"

Lois shifted her arm, and Tacy saw a flash of silver glinting in the light.

"Yes?" Lois said. "And you what?"

Think. Think.

"And I wandered in for a closer look. This place brings back so many memories. I heard you come in, and I would have called out to let you know I was here, but I didn't want you to see me crying."

"Oh, my dear. I know exactly how you feel." Lois turned just enough to reveal the ornate silver letter opener she held in her hand. A smile crested on her face as she set the opener down on the table. "Sometimes it's the little memories that are hardest to bear."

Relief bubbled in Tacy's throat that her excuse had been accepted. But her mouth went dry as Lois's gaze lit upon the open drawer.

A ghost of a frown bent the corners of Lois's lips as she stretched out her long, thin arms and beckoned Tacy forward. "It looks like someone needs a hug. Come here, my dear."

Tacy wiped her damp palms against her jeans and looked toward the door. Surely Lois wouldn't try anything here in her grandfather's office.

Or would she?

Lois closed the gap between them. She pulled Tacy close and squeezed hard.

Wow. Lois is strong. Tacy squirmed sideways and tried pushing back, but Lois's long fingernails dug ridges in her skin.

Oh, that was tight. Too tight.

But just as she was about to cry out in alarm, Lois released her grip.

Tacy recoiled from her grasp. "Thanks. But I think I should head back to the bunkhouse."

"Of course, of course. At the very least, can I offer you a ride?"

"No. I've been looking forward to taking a walk in the fresh air."

Lois didn't seem convinced. "Well, if you insist. But you must promise to have a lie down when you get there. You've had a bit of shock, just like me."

Sucking in a mouthful of air, Tacy turned and walked out of the room.

She rounded the corner and came face-to-face with her reflection in the mirror in the front hall, her face white and her eyes bleary with anxiety and confusion. What had just happened? And why did she feel like she'd barely escaped with her life?

Barge in or wait? Seb was considering his options when Tacy appeared in the doorway and began limping slowly down the drive. He followed behind her, keeping well to the side, hidden behind a border of bushy shrubs, just in case Lois was watching.

Tacy was waiting in the passenger seat of

the truck when he climbed in. He looked at her and shook his head. "I almost lost it when Lois showed up."

"I wonder why she didn't go with my grandfather to Bismarck. It was almost like she knew that something was up. I did manage to find some stuff in the files, so I guess the whole thing was worth it."

Worth it? No. He could only hope that the documents held some answers.

He put on his turn signal and merged onto the main road. "What do you say we stop at Dot's and look at what you found?"

Inside the restaurant, the place was bustling. Customers perched on stools at the counter and crowded the tables facing out toward the street.

Tacy claimed a booth in the back, the one where they used to meet when they were teens. He slid in on the other side of her.

"Like old times, huh?"

Worry lines crisscrossed her forehead, and the set of her mouth revealed her concern. It was a far cry from the happy, hopeful expression she had worn that spring afternoon ten years ago when the two of them met to discuss the future. If memory served, they had been sitting in this same booth when he had proposed the idea that they ought to get married when she turned eighteen.

How strange it was to think back to that moment. They were both so young and immature. He was halfway through his training as an MP and Tacy was a senior in high school, smart and ambitious. But all they could think about was being together, no matter what the stakes.

And there were stakes. Keith Tolbert's plans for Tacy didn't include her getting hitched—especially not to a Hunt. His military service was another strike against him. Keith believed that his daughter was destined for better things than life on an army base, pinching pennies on an enlisted soldier's pay.

But at the time, they felt like Romeo and Juliet. Without the sad ending, of course. And since their families disapproved of them being together, they would have to run away. They'd ask for forgiveness, not permission. The power of their love would soften their parents' hearts, and after a while, everything would be okay.

Seb looked across the table at Tacy. Her eyes were troubled as she recounted her run-in with Lois.

"There was an eerie subtext to our entire conversation. Her words were loving and caring, but she also seemed anxious and suspicious. I had a moment when I imagined that she might just use the letter opener she was holding to stab me in the chest."

What? "Tacy, I should never have let you be the one to…"

"I'm starving. Should we eat first and then look at the papers?" Tacy ran a finger along the laminated menu, looking totally engrossed in the offerings, which was funny since the selection hadn't changed much in the years since she had last been there.

"Sure," he said. "I want a hamburger. How about you?"

"Same," she said.

Once they had placed their orders, he leaned sideways and looked around the restaurant. "Wow. This place is still the same. Is there a spot like it in Denver?"

"No. Dot's is special. But Denver has a lot of good restaurants, and everything's close by, or just a bus ride away. I found a really great place to worship that's only a couple miles from my apartment. How about you?"

Tacy had never been one to be subtle about wanting him to have a relationship with the Lord. But he was touched by how quickly she leaped right in with the question. "I still go to church, if that's what you're asking. For a couple years, I took a break. But then a buddy got me back to reading my Bible, and it all kind of grew from there."

"I'm glad," she said.

"Yeah. I figure that no matter how many times I stumble, God will always be there to offer me a second chance. I think my mom is hoping I'll sign up for one of the small groups that meet on Thursday in the church basement. And, of course, she has big plans for the picnic on Sunday after services."

"Right." The worry lines once again crept across Tacy's forehead.

"What's wrong? I mean, except for the fact that someone is trying to kill you and that you just had a close encounter with our number one suspect."

She smiled, and then her face got serious. "I keep thinking that none of this would have happened if I hadn't agreed to deliver my father's letter. The strange thing is that I don't even know what it said. My grandfather seems to think that it's nothing more than a recital of the same old issues he and my dad argued about before we left. But I don't know. My dad was pretty emotional those last couple weeks."

"He knew he was dying."

"Yeah. I was the one who didn't want to believe it. I always hoped he'd be around to see me try my first case. *He* always said he wanted to be around to see me become a justice on the Supreme Court one day." Tears threatened to fill her eyes, but she held them back. "I know that you always thought he pushed me too hard. But he made so many sacrifices to help me along the way. I can't imagine having a better dad."

Seb took a deep breath. It hurt to see Tacy so broken up when she talked about her father. Even though he and Keith hadn't seen eye to eye in most matters, it was hard to deny the fierceness of Keith's love for his daughter.

A smile wobbled on the sides of her mouth, and a feeling of familiar longing thudded in his chest. This was it, the chance he had been waiting for, the opportunity to continue the conversation they had started while waiting for the rattler to be removed from her car. He still wanted to explain why he had left while she was in the hospital, to lay out all the reasons he had gone back to Texas without talking to her first.

He wanted to explain that he had tried to stay. He had called his CO and begged to extend his leave. But the terror threat level had been raised to red, and all personnel were being ordered to return to base immediately. Keith was supposed to explain all that to Tacy, but did he? Seb knew Keith had held him responsible for their secret marriage, their thoughtless deception, and especially for the decision to go climbing on the cliffs.

But he couldn't blame Keith for everything. The thought of his own ineffectiveness swept against him. Sure, he wrote letters and left messages on Tacy's phone, but his efforts trailed off not long after Tacy and her dad moved to Colorado. For a while, he'd check the flights to Denver and imagine showing up and sweeping Tacy off her feet. But in the end, he always found a reason to stay put. Work filled his hours, and so did the classes he took in his free time to get his degree. When she failed to get in touch, to respond to his messages, he convinced himself that their short marriage been a false start, a mistake that had somehow been rectified without much effort on either of their parts.

He forced himself to smile into Tacy's eyes. "The way things ended between us wasn't right. I'm glad I got the chance to tell you that you'll always be my friend."

He might have said more if the waitress hadn't returned just then with their burgers and fries. He watched Tacy fold her hands to offer a quick prayer of thanksgiving and then take a bite from her sandwich. He wanted to bring the conversation back around to discussing the giant hole she left in his heart when she sent him the divorce papers, but he couldn't find the words, and the moment passed. A strained silence fell between them as they ate.

He finished his burger, and took a long sip of soda. "So, uh, I guess we should look at the papers you grabbed. Anything catch your eye?" His voice sounded forced and too loud.

"Actually, yeah." Tacy set down the fry she was nibbling on and wiped her fingers on the napkin. "I found a purchase agreement, but I can't tell if it is the most current offer."

"Did you recognize the name of the buyer?"

"PTP, Inc. We could check this out at the office of the North Dakota Secretary of State, but we probably can't get their articles of incorporation until Monday. I also found a copy of an old deed." Tacy reached into her backpack and pulled out a crumpled piece of paper. She smoothed it out on the table. "Do you see what it says?" Her finger jabbed at the words on the page.

He leaned closer to read. The document was dated nine years ago, and, if he understood it correctly, Carl seemed to be using it to give Keith a share in the property. He looked up at Tacy, whose eyes were narrowed and thoughtful. He didn't get it. Keith had an interest. But Keith was dead now, so what, if anything, did it mean?

"Even if your Dad is a part owner of the property, how does that affect anything now?"

"Don't you see? It says that the property is conveyed to my grandfather and father as tenants in common."

"You're going to have to help me out here, Tace. I don't understand legal jargon."

"There are two ways to deed property to more than one person. As joint tenants or as tenants in common. Joint tenancy is used mostly for married couples because it includes a right of survivorship for either party. If one of them dies, the ownership of the property is wholly retained by the surviving spouse. But in the case of tenants in common, if one of the parties dies, his ownership in the property passes to his heirs. My father left everything to me. So—"

"You're a partial owner of your grandfather's ranch. Which means that you could benefit from the sale. Or even stop it."

"Not really. What I found in the file is just a copy. For it to have any legal effect, it would have to be recorded. But it doesn't matter either way. I'd never interfere with my grandfather's plans. The ranch is his to do with as he pleases."

"Still, Tacy, it's a pretty good motive for someone wanting you dead."

"Maybe. But who would even know about this?"

He looked at the document again and felt a smile twitch on his face. There was one person who might know.

All he'd need to do is ask.

ELEVEN

On the drive back from Dot's, Tacy slid a glance over toward Seb.

"You okay, Tace?" he asked.

Not okay, but somehow convinced that it was time to make things right between Seb and Timmy. It was pointless to continue to hide the truth from her son. She needed to be practical. There had already been five attempts on her life. If the next one succeeded, Seb would become Timmy's primary caretaker.

But how would Timmy react to the news? Would he be angry? Confused? Upset? Probably all of the above. She stiffened her resolve. It didn't matter. As soon as they got back to the ranch, she'd find a quiet moment to talk to her son.

"I was thinking about what you said at Dot's. About God always being there when we stumble. And I realized that He also offers us a chance to rectify our mistakes. I think it's time to tell Timmy the truth."

"About what?"

"About you being his father."

The pause made it clear that Seb was surprised…but when he spoke again, she couldn't miss the pleased—though cautious—tone in his voice. "I've been on board with that from the start, Tace. You were the one who wanted to keep it a secret. What changed your mind?"

She shrugged. It was a feeling that was difficult to explain.

"How do you want to do it?" Seb pulled to a stop at the bottom of the drive and turned to face her.

"Sandy ought to be back with Timmy at any minute. I'll take a moment alone to talk to him. And then you can join us, and we'll get it all straight, okay?"

"Get it all straight?" Seb raised a brow. "That sounds overly ambitious. Just begin with the truth and see where it goes."

She nearly had a change of heart when Timmy arrived at the bunkhouse. He seemed so happy and innocent—a situation that was bound to change when he found out his mother had kept such an important secret from him. "Did you have fun making cookies?" she asked once Sandy said her goodbyes and headed home.

Seb waited the beat of one second before turning to face Tacy. "That went well," he said.

She shot him a rueful smile. "You're kidding, right?" Timmy's reaction had been so offhanded, almost blasé, compared to what she had been expecting.

"Yeah. I thought he'd say more. He probably needs time to get used to the idea. I assume you told him that I would have done a better job of being a dad if I had known."

She was disappointed that he needed to ask. "Of course."

"I guess that's it, then. Now I suppose you'll want to call your grandfather and give him the news. Better for him to find out from you than to hear it through the grapevine."

Seb was right. There was no good reason to continue to delay. She picked up her phone and walked into the bedroom. Her hand shook as she punched in the number. Her grandfather answered on the first ring.

"Grandfather. How did it go at the doctor's today?"

"My numbers are good, so I won't complain."

"I'm glad to hear it. Listen. Um. While you were gone, I…um stopped by the house to pick something up and ran into Lois. I thought she was going with you to Bismarck."

"So did I. But apparently, there was some sort of crisis at the flower stop."

Oddly coincidental, but what could she say? "Okay. I was also calling for another reason. There's something I wanted to tell you when you dropped me off early this morning, but we were both so exhausted that I decided to wait for another day." *Say it. Don't dance around it. Say it, and it will be over, just like that.* "Seb and I got married when I was eighteen."

"What?"

"Seb Hunt and I got married when I turned eighteen."

"You got married to one of the Hunts? How is that possible?"

A flush of warmth rose in her cheeks. "Seb was there for me when my mom left. He was a friend first, but, over time, he became something more."

Her grandfather blew a long breath through his nose. "And no one knew about this? What about the Hunts? Were they aware of this secret? It's all so hard to understand. Did this marriage take place before or after you moved to Colorado?"

"Before. I know it was an impulsive thing to do. But we loved each other and wanted to be together. But then I had the accident. And Seb's leave ran out, and he had to get back to his base in Texas."

She took a deep breath. She had gotten through the first part. Now she needed to tell him the rest.

"You mean that boy left you when you were in the hospital? Disgraceful!"

Disgraceful seemed like too harsh a word to describe Seb's behavior, given his duty to the military, but her grandfather's reaction wasn't far off the mark from how she'd felt at the time. "Once we were separated, we…couldn't seem to find our way back to each other," she said as diplomatically as she could. "So, we thought that the best thing for both of us would be to end things quietly and move on."

Her grandfather's sigh was loud and exasperated. "That's why you and Keith left, isn't it? To get you away from Sebastian Hunt? I should have known. It all comes back to the Hunts."

"Well, whether you like it or not, you're going to have to get used to dealing with the Hunts. Because when I woke up in the hospital after the accident, I found out I was pregnant. Seb and I have a little boy. His name is Timmy, and he's nine. Seb didn't know about Timmy either. None of the Hunts did. My dad and I didn't mean to hurt anyone by hiding the truth, but since I've been back, I realized it was a mistake."

There was a long silence. Ten seconds passed, and she began to wonder. Had her grandfather hung up, or was he still on the line, listening?

He cleared his throat and reestablished the connection. "When can I meet my great-grandson?" he said.

Seb couldn't hear much of Tacy's conversation with her grandfather through the bedroom door. And try as he might, it was impossible to predict Carl Tolbert's reaction to the news that he had a nine-year-old great-grandson he had never met. There was already so much bad blood between their two families. Would Timmy's presence make things better or worse?

It was hard to say. He remembered the list he had made that morning of tasks he hoped to accomplish before the end of the day. He unfolded the piece of paper and glanced down at the items printed on the page.

1. Make a list of pros and cons concerning the job offer in DC.
2. Help replace the sprinkler.
3. Talk to GG.

A couple of weeks earlier, before Tacy arrived on the scene, he had been thinking that a change of scenery might be a good idea. He loved the ranch, but a new job would bring all sorts of interesting challenges and give him the opportunity to hone the skills he had acquired in the military. But the more he thought about it, the less he was sure that a move to DC would be a good thing—for him or for Timmy.

"What do you think, Cody?" He reached down to pet the six-month-old springer spaniel tangled around his legs. "Should I turn down the job or take it?"

Cody thumped his tail twice.

Was that a yes or a no?

Maybe he needed to punt on the decision, at least for the moment. He glanced down to the last two items on the list. Before he spoke to Gunnar Graff, he wanted to get his father's advice about the best way to approach the attorney. Which meant heading out to the north field to help fix the sprinkler.

He called Steven and asked him to keep an eye on Tacy and Timmy. "On my way, bro," Steven said. He hung up the phone as Tacy came out of the bedroom, her eyes leaking tears.

"My grandfather's really angry that I waited so long to tell him about Timmy. Not that I blame him. Oh, Seb. I really mucked this whole thing up. I just wish I could do it all over and start with the truth."

He did, too. That's what they needed, a trip

back in time so he and Tacy could forgo their decision to climb Shepherd's Peak and head straight for his base in Texas. He'd be right there with her when they found out about the pregnancy, and if their baby was a girl or a boy. And he'd be with her in the delivery room when Timmy was born.

The bunkhouse door slammed with a loud clatter. Steven. Seb waited for him to get settled and then fired up his truck and headed to the north field.

He might as well have been crossing a desert with the waves of heat shimmering across the fields. Once his truck thumped over the cattle guard that separated the road from the grassland, he rolled down the window and inhaled the scent of dry hay baking in the scorching sun. The irrigation system didn't work well even in the best of times. But the high temperatures of the past month had quadrupled the demand for water, so it was hardly surprising when problems with the sprinkler system occurred.

He spotted his father's SUV on the side of the road. He pulled in behind it and walked across the field to join him.

"I came to help." he said.

"Thanks," his dad said. "I'll show you the problem."

It took them a half hour to find the crack in

the central pivot point of the piping. After that, the rest was easy.

His dad clapped a hand on his back. "I'm off to check out a problem at the south gate. You want to come along and take a look?"

"I wish I could. But I'm thinking of driving into town to talk to Gunnar Graff about an issue that might affect the sale of the Tolbert ranch."

"Two words. Be careful. I've seen him in court when the gloves come off. Behind that polished demeanor, the man has the instincts of a street fighter."

Seb waited for his dad to drive off before he pulled out his phone to call the law firm of Graff and Klein to ask for an appointment. The receptionist asked if he could he make it into the office by five, which gave him just enough time to change his shirt and drive into town.

He arrived minutes before his appointment. A blonde receptionist stood by the front desk, twirling a set of car keys, clearly ready to leave for the day. He followed her directions to the first office at the end of the hall.

Gunnar looked up from his computer and waved him in. "I'm just finishing up. Grab a seat, and I'll be with you in a minute."

Seb folded himself into one of the chairs in front of the desk and took out his phone. It looked like his pal from the FBI had left him another message. He was about to pull it up when Gunnar closed his laptop and leaned across his desk. "So, young man. What can I do for you today?"

"I don't want to waste too much of your time, so I'll cut to the chase. I'd like to talk to you about the Tolbert ranch."

"Right. You were there the other night when your brother made that scene at the dining room table. He's obviously passionate about saving bulls. But I'm still operating on the assumption that the sale will proceed as expected. I don't really know how it has anything to do with you. It is Carl's business, and no one else's."

"Are you sure?" He narrowed his eyes.

Gunnar drummed his fingers on his desk and returned his stare. A few seconds ticked by. "It seems like there is something you want to say. Let's pass on the theatrics. Tell me what's on your mind."

Trust Gunnar to not fall for any intimidation act. His father's words played across his mind. The instincts of a street fighter. Well, two could play at the game. He reached into his pocket and pulled out the document that Tacy had found earlier in the day. He laid it on Gunnar's desk, smoothing out the wrinkles. "Do you recognize this? You should, considering it is your name at the bottom as notary."

The surge of satisfaction he had expected was short-lived. Gunnar was poker-faced as he picked up the piece of paper, scanned it and set it down on the desk.

"Sure, I remember. I'm curious as to how it fell into your hands. Carl Tolbert isn't one for sharing information, especially with a Hunt. I am not certain why you're showing it to me."

Anger welled inside his chest, but he held on to his temper. He crossed his arms. "Well, according to this deed, Tacy Tolbert has an ownership interest in the property."

"Are you accusing me of trying to deny my goddaughter her inheritance?" Gunnar spoke in a flippant tone, but Seb noticed the vein pulsing in his neck. So, he had struck a nerve. Good. Gunnar glared at him, and he glared right back. "If so, your accusation is moot." Gunnar slid the paper across the desk. "Not that it is any of your business, but Carl asked me to draft this deed about a year after Keith left for Colorado. He wanted to make a good faith effort by offering him more of a say in the ranch, hoping to entice him back to North Dakota. As his lawyer, I recommended that we send the original document to be recorded so that it had full legal effect, but Carl wanted to put the ball into Keith's hands. As you can see, this is a copy. And it was not recorded. Keith saw it as a hollow gesture, meant to guilt him into returning to North Dakota. He claimed to have burned the document right after he received it."

Gunnar shrugged. "So that was that. With the original destroyed, no conveyance took place. I honestly doubt Carl was all that surprised. Much as I, personally, would like for Tacy to be a part of the sale transaction, the fact of the matter is that she has no legal standing. The ranch belongs to Carl, in full. Now," Gunnar stood up. "I don't appreciate you coming in here and accusing me of acting in any underhanded way. I didn't need to share any of this information, but Tacy is my best friend's daughter. I've told you all of this in confidence so we can put this whole matter to rest. But I don't wish to discuss my clients or their business with you ever again."

Seb pushed himself up from his chair. Anger and frustration burned in his chest. He had come here prepared to get the better of Gunnar Graff, and now he was being sent away, chastened, discouraged and humiliated.

But most of all, he was worried. If Gunnar was right and the deed had been destroyed, then they were back at square one when it came to finding a motive for the attacks on Tacy. And with no idea who was after her or why, there was no way to tell when the would-be killer would strike again.

TWELVE

Tacy was physically exhausted and ready for bed. Dinner at the Hunts' had been followed by a rousing game of *Sorry* and a trip to the stables to groom the horses. By the time they trudged back to the bunkhouse and Timmy was tucked in tight, she was looking forward to curling up under a blanket and calling it a night. Morning would bring its own set of challenges.

She and Timmy were going to meet her grandfather at Dot's for breakfast. The three of them would have some time together, but her grandfather was sure to have questions she'd prefer not to answer in front of Timmy. After an hour, Seb would pick up Timmy, giving her and her grandfather some time alone.

Was it any wonder that she had woken up anxious and upset? She was still fretting when she pulled into the lot behind Dot's.

Timmy must have realized that she was stalling. "What are we waiting for, Mom? Why don't we go into the restaurant? I'm starving."

She turned sideways to look at him. "You remember how it felt last year at the championship, when you were up at bat in the last inning, with two men on and the chance to win the game?"

Timmy nodded. "That was a lot of pressure."

"That's right. You knew what you had to do, but also that it was going to be really hard. That's how I feel now. I didn't let anyone in Chimney Bluff know when you were born. Last night, when I told my grandfather about you, I realized that my decision had caused an ache in his heart that might never go away. And now I'm stuck, not knowing how I can fix that."

Timmy reached forward and patted her shoulder. "I'll help you, Mom. Maybe I can talk about my baseball team. Do you think your grandfather would like to hear about some of our games?"

From the mouth of babes. "I'm sure he would. Hey. We better get inside before they run out of pancakes. Now, that would really be a disaster of epic proportions."

Her grandfather's eyes pegged hers before they even made it into the restaurant. Timmy must have noticed, too, because he reached over and took her hand as she raised her palm to wave.

"Is that him?" Timmy asked. "He looks like grandpa Keith, but older and with a lot more hair. Don't worry, Mom. You'll hit a home run. It'll be okay."

Timmy was right. For the most part, anyway.

"Nice to meet you, young man," Her grandfather stood up and held out his right hand. With a solemn face, Timmy extended out his own arm. Tacy blinked back the unexpected tears that had formed in her eyes, watching her little boy shake hands with her grandfather.

The three of them took their seats, and an awkward silence fell between them.

"Timmy learned to ride horses at camp." Tacy scrambled to find a way to jumpstart the conversation.

"Is that so," her grandfather replied.

"Yep. I'd always wanted to learn how to ride, and Grampa Keith promised to teach me. But then he got sick, so he couldn't. He did take me camping so I already know how canoe and fish. The best part about camp was swimming. There was a tire swing in the river. Can you believe it? Have you ever seen a swing over water before?"

Her grandfather blinked. "I can't say that I have."

"We also got to see lots of animals at camp. There were the horses, of course. But we also saw deer, and my friend Michael claimed he saw a moose. I really like animals. Especially dogs. They're my favorite." Timmy turned toward her. "Mom, did you have a dog growing up?"

Tacy shook her head and opened her mouth to reply no, but her grandfather interrupted her.

"No. No pet dogs, at least. But we always had one or two border collies around the property."

"Really? Cool!"

And so it went, Timmy's artless chatter putting all of them at ease. Her grandfather was clearly delighted by his great-grandson, peppering him with questions about school and camp and life in Colorado. Timmy's natural exuberance was the perfect foil to her grandfather's gruffness. The two of them might have talked for hours if her grandfather hadn't suddenly pushed himself up from the booth and reached over to shake Timmy's hand.

"It's been very nice to meet you, young man, but I'm afraid I have to head back to the ranch to deal with a problem with one of our mares."

Tacy snuck a glance at the clock on the wall over the counter. It was only ten thirty.

"Can't you stay a bit longer, Grandfather?" she asked.

"I'm sorry, my dear. I can't. I had already arranged for the vet to meet me at the stables."

"Will I see you at the church picnic?"

"No. Lois and I have other plans."

She drew her grandfather into a tight hug. "Another time, then."

"I'm glad I got to meet Timmy."

She was, too.

She took a moment to text Seb about the change in the plan. Breakfast ended earlier than expected. Headed back to the bunkhouse. See you soon.

On the way to the car, disappointment gave way to relief. Her grandfather seemed to have forgiven her. And he had been genuinely pleased to meet and talk to Timmy.

As she turned her key in the ignition, the brake light on the dashboard flashed red. That was odd. And annoying. It hadn't been on during her drive into town.

It was probably just a glitch in the electrical system. Wasn't there a gas station at the bottom of the hill, half a block away? She'd stop there and ask one of the mechanics to check it out.

Halfway down Main, she pumped the brakes. The pedal felt squishy, like an old balloon half filled with sand. And the car didn't slow down. She gulped down the lump of anxiety in her throat. She probably just needed to apply more force to get the brakes to engage.

She slammed her foot down harder, but the pedal flapped uselessly under the sole of her shoe. Panic threaded through her veins. She was moving faster now, headed toward the bottom of the hill. Her stomach roiled at she shot past Lois's flower shop and blew through a stop sign at Third and Vine.

There were no pedestrians or other cars at the intersection. *Thank you, God.* Her fingers clenched the gear shift and pressed it into First, but even that didn't slow her momentum. Neither did her desperate yanking on the emergency brake. There was nothing left to do but pray for a flat stretch of road, long enough for her to slow down.

Tacy's Nissan swooshed past Seb on the other side of the road, driving way too fast, at least ten miles over the limit. He craned his neck and looked behind him. Her car had already disappeared from his sight. He twisted the wheel into a tight turn, pressed down on the accelerator, and raced to catch up with Tacy, certain something was wrong.

He pressed a button on the console. "Call Tacy," he said.

She picked up on the first ring.

"Seb. My brakes aren't working."

"Did you try shifting down to low gear?"

"It didn't work. And I pulled the emergency brake, but it only engaged for a second."

What else? What else? Think, think. Panic was clouding his judgment.

"Okay. You need to get somewhere flat to slow your momentum. In about a half mile, you'll come to a fork in the road. Go left, and the pavement will level out. Let's see if that helps in reducing your speed. When the car stops moving, try to force it into Park. I'll be right behind you. But let's keep the line open just in case."

"Timmy's here with me." Tacy's voice was tight with anxiety.

"I know, Tace. You're doing great. Just a little bit longer, and you'll come to the split. Go left. Remember."

"Left," she repeated.

"Okay, then." he said. *Please, God. Let this work.*

His training had taught him not to jump to conclusions. But there was no way this brake failure was just a coincidence.

Regret battered his conscience. He had promised to protect Tacy and Timmy. But now they were on a collision course with vehicles ahead of them on the road, and there was nothing he could do but pray.

He kept a few yards behind Tacy as she approached the split. But up ahead, beyond the curve snaked a line of slow-moving traffic.

"Tace, go right," he said. "Go right."

Too late.

She went left.

Tacy's voice cracked on the console. "Seb. There's a truck about twenty yards in front of me that's barely moving. I'm heading off the road. Hold on, Timmy. This could be rough." Her voice faded as Timmy chattered in the background. Something about Snowy, the mare he was planning to ride that afternoon.

The Nissan bumped off the tarmac and dived into the gully, thumping straight down into a wide field of sunflowers.

He stuck like glue behind the runaway vehicle. His speed clocked at twenty as he followed the Nissan down the embankment. *Fifteen, ten, five.* Thick green stalks bent sideways and scattered in their wake. Mustard-colored petals and black seed pods rained through the air as Tacy's car finally bumped to a halt against a crowd of bowing flower heads.

Seb pushed aside a tall plant that had been sheared of its leaves as he edged open the truck's door. Ten feet in front of him, Tacy stepped out of her vehicle.

A dozen or so people jumped out of cars and stumbled down the embankment, almost all with cell phones stuck to their ears. The owner of the field arrived on an ATV. He didn't seem bothered that a portion of his crop was destroyed. He just wanted to make sure that everyone was okay.

Thank You, God. They are.

Its red lights flashing, a patrol car screeched to a halt on the shoulder of the road, followed closely behind by an ambulance and a tow truck. As the sheriff bolted out of his car and headed toward Tacy, Seb nudged Timmy to a quiet corner of the field so as not to eavesdrop on what was being said.

"You okay?" he asked once they were far enough away from the commotion.

Timmy nodded. "Do you think we can still go riding this afternoon?"

Hmm. They'd have to see how Tacy felt about that.

"Why wouldn't the car stop?" Timmy asked.

"I'm not sure. I think it had something to do with the brakes."

Timmy nodded. "That's what I think, too."

Frustration clawed at his senses. Would this nightmare ever end? The thought of what might have happened was too dire to even contemplate.

Fifteen minutes later, the show was over. The car was towed, the statements had been taken. Even the sheriff was gone.

Tacy walked over to where they were standing.

"What did the sheriff say?" he asked. He had kept his composure during the crisis, but seeing Tacy so drawn and vulnerable caused his heart to hammer in his chest.

Tacy looked at Timmy. She seemed to recognize the need to choose her words with care. "He said he'd get the report from the mechanic, and he'd follow through from there."

Timmy scooted into the space between them, "Mom, I'm really sorry the brakes are messed up on your car. But can we still go riding this afternoon? Please."

"We'll see, okay?" Tacy said.

Timmy reached over and patted her hand. "Okay. But when we get back, we should see if Steven needs help in the stables. I want Snowy to get used to me, just in case we do end up going for that ride."

Seb could see the love in Tacy's eyes as she smiled down at Timmy. He knew where she was coming from. It wasn't easy saying no to Timmy. But whoever had tampered with the brakes of Tacy's Nissan had raised the stakes. And now every decision they made going forward would be marked by one immutable goal.

Keep Timmy safe at all costs.

THIRTEEN

Seb pulled his chair in toward the table so Tacy could scoot by him to answer a call. She walked to the next room and leaned against the wall. From what he could hear of her side of the conversation, she seemed to be talking to the mechanic at the shop.

His mom must have been eavesdropping too because when Tacy returned to the dining room, she voiced her dismay. "Is everything okay with your car, hon?"

Tacy shook her head. "No. There's quite a bit of damage to the suspension system, and it looks like they need to replace the brakes."

Timmy perked right up. "Seb was right, Mom. He said that was why you weren't able to stop."

Seb looked across the table and met Tacy's glance.

He waited until they were cleaning up in the kitchen to find out more.

"The mechanic doesn't think it was an accident." Tacy's eyes looked haunted as she plunged her hands into the sudsy water in the sink. "The whole time he was explaining it to me, I kept picturing someone crawling under my car and cutting the lines while Timmy and I were in Dot's. I parked in the back lot, so there weren't any cameras that might have caught the person responsible."

Seb opened the dishwasher and began to stack the glassware on the top rack. "There's no way you could have expected someone to tamper with your brakes." But *he* should have expected it. Tacy's assailant was resourceful and quick to press for the advantage. And the sight of her Nissan in a crowded, unsupervised lot must had been too tempting a target to ignore.

She turned to him, her eyes brimming with tears. "Timmy was in the car with me, Seb. He would have died if we hadn't chanced upon that field."

It took all his strength not to reach out and pull Tacy into the shelter of his arms. The possibility of finding his son only to lose him was too horrific to contemplate. "I'm certain the sheriff will check the brake line for prints. But so far, the person targeting you has been smart enough to avoid leaving any trace. Let's just hang around close to home for the rest of the day."

"But I promised Timmy that we'd go riding this afternoon."

Why? he wanted to ask. But he knew why. The answer was front and center when he arrived at the corral. His gut clenched at the sight of his son sitting proud and tall in Snowy's saddle, beaming with joy. To further tug at his heartstrings, Timmy was wearing a beat-up pair of old boots and a dented cowboy hat that looked suspiciously like something he had worn when he was nine.

He walked over toward Steven, who was grooming Topper.

"Looks like we're really doing this." Steven said. "Tacy told me what happened with her car."

"We just need to watch both of them like hawks."

"Roger that."

They started off in pairs. Seb rode Chief and stuck next to Timmy while Steven was on Topper and Tacy rode Lizzie.

Seb kept a tight hold on Chief's reins to keep pace with Snowy. He didn't usually like to talk while riding, but Timmy wanted to chat about school, especially his favorite parts, gym and recess.

What had his dad said when he first met Timmy? *The apple doesn't fall far from the tree.* It was amazing to hear Timmy describe the things he loved to do—play baseball, watch baseball and play soccer. It sounded like a list he might have made when he was nine. Before he got interested in girls.

Well, one girl in particular. Tacy.

"Seb?" Tacy turned around and cocked her head sideways. "Left or right?"

"Left." He pointed toward the creek.

This was nice. Even though the sun was hot and bright, the day was perfect for a long, easy ride. The plan was to do a quick tour of the Hunts' property and then to cross over to the Tolberts' so that Timmy could see where Tacy had grown up.

He squinted against the glare of the sun. Sparse clumps of brown grass dotted the landscape. Off in the distance, the cliffs rose up abruptly and then, further along the horizon, there was a cluster of small pine-covered hills.

What would Timmy think of the land? To Seb, it was home, beautiful in its severe, unyielding way. But to a kid born and raised against the majestic beauty of the Rocky Mountains? It seemed unlikely this setting would hold much appeal.

He cut another glance Timmy's way. Was his saddle secure? Was Snowy pulling at the reins?

This had to be the downside of being a parent. The fresh worries and endless concern. Timmy didn't seem to notice as he concentrated on remaining upright in the saddle, his body hunched forward, his fingers griping the reins, a smile of satisfaction creased across his face. The beginnings of a matching smile played on Seb's lips. This was his son. And they were riding together across the fields. Timmy gave a gentle pull against Snowy's reins as the mare began to veer to the side, and Seb's smile grew into a grin. Timmy's focus reminded him of his own resoluteness, not that it was needed. Snowy was about as docile as a horse could be.

Up ahead, Steven and Tacy slowed and waited for them to catch up.

Steven looked at Seb and pointed toward the sky. "You sure you want to give all this up? I couldn't do it. No way. Move to Washington, DC? No thank you."

Uh-oh. Seb grimaced. He hadn't found the chance to discuss his job offer with Tacy. Not that it was a secret, or that he needed her permission, but he wanted to wait until… What had he been waiting for? He cast a glance Tacy's direction and read the surprise in her eyes.

"Hey, Steven," he called, pulling up on his reins. "You ride up front with Timmy, okay? I'm going to fall back and talk to Tace."

"Sure thing." Steven muttered as he trotted forward, "Sorry if I said something I shouldn't have." His face was the picture of innocence, but Seb knew his brother well enough to be suspicious. Not that he would claim malicious intent. Just Steven being Steven.

Tacy cantered up next to him.

He waited until their horses synched their pace before turning to face her.

"I should have said something sooner, but a couple weeks ago, I was offered a job with the FBI in Washington, DC. I'm not a hundred percent sure I'm going to take it. But no matter what, you don't need to worry. Timmy will always be my top priority, no matter where I go."

Tacy nodded, but her clenched jaw and rigid shoulders suggested she was upset. He wanted to be upfront with her, to be able to talk about the options available to both of them. But at the moment, she seemed too closed off for that kind of conversation.

He shook his head, determined to reclaim the pleasant feelings he had been experiencing just moments before. It was still a beautiful day. The gentle gait of Chief beneath his legs was familiar and soothing. They were following the trail to the old mine. It used to be one of his favorite treks, although he hadn't ridden it in years.

The mine wasn't really a mine anymore. It was more like an abandoned cave that had closed for decades. But that rusty metal link fence hadn't been enough to deter him and Steven and Tacy. Still, he wasn't sure he wanted his nine-year-old son following in those particular footsteps.

"Hey, Steven. Let's go a bit further and then turn around."

They arrived at the river. With the summer being so dry, it was little more than a trickle. The sight of the water burbling between the barren fields filled him with a pang of nostalgia. Part of him wished that he could be like Steven, throw caution to the wind, and pretend that he was a teenager again. But the woman on the horse beside him was a stark reminder of how much things had changed. Back in the old days, Tacy would have been galloping ahead, her long hair billowing behind her. Now her mare kept a steady walk and her face looked set in stone.

"Let's stop at the bluffs and then head for home," he said to his brother.

He cast another glance at Tacy. His mind raced as he tried to come up with ways to restart the conversation, but everything he thought of seemed trite. Several yards ahead of them, Steven and Timmy had followed the river beyond the bend toward the rocks and then disappeared from sight.

A tingle of apprehension slid up his spine. Now he remembered why he didn't ride this trail anymore. The river. The rocks. They brought back memories of Tacy's accident. He spurred Chief faster. He wanted eyes on Timmy. Now.

Bam!

The blast of a shotgun exploded in the air. Beneath him, Chief tensed and pushed into a gallop. Adrenaline hummed through Seb's body as he raced around the curve.

His stomach dropped.

A hundred yards ahead, he could see Snowy, careening across the field with Timmy clutching his neck and Steven riding hard behind them.

He yanked on Chief's reins and charged forward.

A coil of fear tightened in Tacy's chest. Her anger toward Seb evaporated, forgotten as dread washed over her.

With shaking hands, she pulled on Lizzie's reins, bringing the heaving horse to a halt. Lizzie didn't have the swiftness or stamina to catch up with the three riders galloping across the field. She watched as Seb drew alongside Snowy and then exhaled in an uneven whoosh as Snowy picked up speed and veered to the left. Watching the two brothers galloping after her son, their bodies low and flattened against their horses' backsides, she felt powerless. And she hated that emotion. It was the same feeling she had experienced when her mother and father used to argue. But this was so much worse. Sharper. Deeper. Shattering.

Pray.

The word echoed straight from her heart into her brain. She might not be able to stop Snowy, but she could entreat the One who could. She blew out a deep breath, her eyes still trained on her son, her mind alert to every movement of the chase, as her soul silently implored God. *Help him. Please.*

She leaned forward against Lizzie's neck to get a better view. Seb drew up alongside Snowy again, and this time Steven mirrored him on the other side. In unison, the brothers reached forward and pulled on Snowy's reins. The panicked animal shook his head, his mane dancing wildly, as if to show his resistance.

And then, finally, Snowy slowed to a canter. And then a trot. And then a full stop. Tacy urged Lizzie forward, slipping off her horse as soon as she reached the three riders, her arms wrapping around Timmy. Tears prickled at the back of her eyes as she held on for dear life. She turned toward Steven and Seb and mouthed her thanks. Both men were breathing heavily, their hats pushed back on their heads and their hair damp with sweat.

"Mom! Mom! Did you see that?" Timmy's

high voice broke the silence. He pulled out of her embrace. His brown eyes looked huge in his pale face, but there was excitement and eagerness in his expression. "It felt like I was flying."

Steven snorted. "Yeah, who even knew that Snowy could move that fast?"

"Timmy?" Tacy looked at her son.

"I'm okay, Mom. Snowy got spooked at that loud noise. But I held on."

"You sure did." Seb ruffled his hair and then exhaled deeply. "But I think that's enough excitement for one day. If we cut across the fields, we're not too far from home. Let's walk, and give these horses a break." He picked up Chief's and Snowy's reins. Beside him, Timmy continued talking excitedly about the race, but Tacy recognized a weariness in Seb's gait.

She turned to face Steven.

"Thank you," she said.

Steven had been watching his brother as well, but now he turned his gaze toward Tacy. "You don't need to thank me. I would have done it for anyone. It's the way things are out here. You watch out for your neighbors. And it's not like Timmy is just anyone."

Point taken. Steven's words made her feel small. "Who do you think fired the shotgun?" she asked.

"I didn't see anything," Steven said. "The

blast could have come from the mine or a nearby field. But this is North Dakota. Shotguns are a part of life here."

She nodded. She understood what he was trying to say. Not everything that happened was about her or whoever was targeting her.

She looked toward Seb and Timmy.

Steven followed her gaze. "Don't break his heart again, Tace. You really messed him up when you asked for the divorce."

What? She narrowed her eyes and shook her head. Steven had it wrong. She wasn't the one who had filed for divorce—it was Seb who had sent her the paperwork. Seb who hadn't been willing to give their marriage a chance.

Why would Seb have told his brother such a blatant lie?

FOURTEEN

You really messed him up when you asked for the divorce. Steven's words played across her mind the rest of the day and into the night. But as morning dawned, she vowed to let go of them. If Seb had misrepresented the facts to his family, it was up to him to set the record straight. Besides, it was the start of a new day. Timmy was still sleeping, and she was looking forward to enjoying a moment of peace.

She carried her coffee out to the porch and settled back on the wicker rocking chair to watch the sunrise over the pasture.

How amazing that God had blessed the world with this beautiful creation.

She sat for a while, thinking and rocking. Hard to believe, but it was almost a week ago that she had arrived in Chimney Bluff to deliver her dad's letter. And yet she had failed to complete that simple task.

Nothing had turned out the way she expected.

A worried frown bent the corner of her lips. From the moment he had ridden to her rescue with the bison, Seb had continually risked his life to protect her. He was brave and selfless. And he was proving to be a great father to Timmy. Seeing them together caused an extra little flutter in her heart.

Was that why she was so hurt to hear that Seb might take a job in Washington, DC? She had allowed herself to imagine that he would stay in Chimney Bluff or, in her wildest dreams, move to Denver to be near his son. But it was his life and his decision. He didn't need to run his plans by her. She didn't get a vote in what he did with his life. And she didn't want one…did she?

When had everything become so complicated? The danger and the emotional upheaval of the past week had sent her emotions cartwheeling and caused her to question many of the decisions she had made in the past. She found herself wondering what would have happened if she and Seb had found a way to talk things through after the accident. Would they have worked out their differences and stayed together to become a family?

A flush of heat warmed her cheeks. It didn't matter. Seb had been as ready to move on then as he was today. She needed to focus on getting back to Denver.

A rumble of distant thunder interrupted her musings. Her eyes scanned the clouds in the eastern sky. Were storms in the forecast for the day ahead? Everyone said that they needed the rain, but not on the day of the church picnic. With the number of outdoor activities planned, it might well be postponed if the weather didn't cooperate. Which, come to think of it, might not be such a bad thing since Seb had failed in his efforts to convince Timmy that it would be a lot more fun to skip the picnic and stay home and play games. But in the end, they had both made the call that they would go.

She settled back in the rocker and closed her eyes. But her moment of solitude came to an end as the screen door creaked open on its hinges. Her heart swelled at the sight of her little boy, the bottoms of *Star Wars* pajamas hitched up high above his waist. Standing next to Timmy, Seb managed to radiate security and contentment with his quiet confidence, manly scuff and rumpled dark hair.

"Mornin'," he said, his voice gravelly with sleep.

Boom. Was that her heart drumming in her chest? Maybe this indifference deal was going to be harder than she thought.

Father and son announced they were both hungry for breakfast. As if on cue, Sandy appeared, carrying a basket of muffins, with Scott and Steven following close behind.

Everyone settled down to discuss the weather and the likelihood that the picnic would still take place. Sandy put an end to the debate by calling the woman in charge, who had decided against postponement. After services, volunteers would set up the tables and chairs in the field behind the church. If the showers materialized as expected, the gathering would be moved inside to the hall.

Timmy wasn't pleased by the notion of a plan B. "Seb says that if it rains, we'll have to play bingo in the hall."

"You don't like bingo?" She hoisted a dented tin ice chest into the bed of Seb's truck. "Don't worry, Timmy. The showers are supposed to hold off until the evening, at least according to the app on my phone."

"Seb says we need the percipa…percipa-ta-tion."

"Seb is right. He usually is about the weather."

"What's that?" Seb ambled over to where they were standing, his mouth tugged into a wide grin. "Who's trying to tease me about my interest in the weather?"

Timmy curled his fingers into a fist and rapped them twice against the truck. "Hey, Seb. Knock, knock."

"Who's there?"

"Bee Eye."

Seb raised a brow. "Bee Eye, who?"

"Bee Eye, N-G-O, and Bingo was his name, oh." Timmy collapsed in hysterics.

"Good one, Timmy," Seb said. "Hey, what do you say you go inside and see if there's any more stuff to load up for the picnic?"

"Sure thing," Timmy said. "I'll ask Scott and Sandy."

Scott and Sandy? It was still early days, but at some point, Timmy needed to start calling Seb Dad and referring to Seb's parents as Grandma and Grandpa.

"Can I talk to you a minute, Tace?" Seb said.

"Sure." She pulled herself up on the truck's open gate and waited for Seb to continue.

He cleared his throat. "Yesterday, when Steven mentioned the job offer in DC, I saw the look on your face. I'm sorry you had to hear about it that way. I wanted to say more then, but it didn't seem like the right time or place."

She nodded. She could do this. She could act like she didn't care. "We'll find a way to make it work, no matter what you decide."

"But it's something we should discuss if we're going to share custody of Timmy."

Share custody?

He looked at her expectantly. "I realize that

there are still loose ends that need to be tied up. But no matter what happens, we both want what's best for Timmy."

Wait. Seb seemed to be getting ahead of himself here. She was willing to discuss a visitation schedule. But shared custody? She wanted to argue against it—loudly and right away—but there was no point in overreacting. She needed to calmly and rationally convince Seb that it would be a mistake to shuffle Timmy between two households. No. It would be more than a mistake. It would be a disaster.

"And, Tace, remember. Timmy's my top priority here. I'm making up for lost time of not knowing I had a son."

She sighed. What Seb said was true. But she wasn't the only one who had made mistakes. No matter what he told his family, he was the one who had given up on their marriage and filed for divorce. But she didn't want to resort to pointing fingers and laying blame. Not today. Maybe not ever. "Why uproot Timmy from everyone and everything he loves? Kids need stability, Seb. Not two different schools with two different teachers and two different sets of classmates."

Seb's eyes reflected a hardened glint. "Fine. I'll be the one who provides the stability. I missed out on nine years, Tacy. That's a hundred and eight months. So, does that mean I get the next hundred and eight months of sole custody?"

She took a deep breath as she struggled to maintain her civility. Just like that, all her good will evaporated at the memory of the hurt and sadness of the past ten years.

Her dad had known this would happen. He had predicted it would be a huge mistake to tell Seb that he had a son. And now, look how quickly it had all gone off the rails. One minute, she and Seb were bonding as friends, and the next, he was conniving to get the upper hand in a custody agreement.

"You left me, Seb. I was the one in the hospital. I kept asking everyone where you were, but no one would answer. Imagine how it felt to discover that you had gone back to Texas without even saying goodbye. I realize that you didn't know about Timmy. But when you got on that plane, you turned your back on every part of our old life together."

"That's ridiculous, Tacy, and you know it. I didn't have any choice. My leave had run out, and if I'd stayed longer, I'd have been considered AWOL. And let's be fair here. I came back as soon as I could. But by that time, you were gone. I tried to reach out to you. But you wouldn't even take the time to tell me that you were okay."

"And that was enough for you to throw in the towel and file for divorce?"

"*You* sent me the paperwork, which—incidentally—arrived the day I returned after three weeks of hard duty in the field."

She shook her head. "No. That's wrong. I remember it clearly because I was back in the hospital in Denver, being treated for an infection in my leg, when my dad brought the documents for me to sign as you requested."

A muscle tightened in Seb's jaw. "That is not how it happened. But it's exactly what I would have expected of your dad. But not of you. You should have known better. You should have trusted that I would never hurt you like that."

Could what Seb was saying be true? Was he really not the one who had initiated the paperwork for the divorce? But then, how…why? She closed her eyes and shook her head. Even if he was being honest, that didn't let him off the hook for not being there when she needed him. That second time she had been in the hospital had been a dark time for her. She had barely the energy to make it through each day. When her dad handed her the paperwork, she had scrawled her name on the dotted line and then retreated back into a tight cocoon of loneliness and pain. Maybe she should have made a greater effort to read the documents before she signed, but she was in a pretty compromised state as it was, pregnant, drifting in and out of consciousness as the doctors pumped meds into her system, trying to keep her alive.

And did it even matter who had wanted the divorce? Even if her dad had overstepped his parental role, that didn't negate the fact that Seb had abandoned her of his own free will. Seb. Her best friend. The one person in the whole world who knew the deep ache and guilt she felt when her mom walked out of her life. She could still remember the heavy loneliness that had been her constant companion during her weeks in the hospital. But then it felt like God had understood her distress because she wasn't alone. There was someone with her, her tiny baby who was growing and kicking and relying on her to stay strong and get well. That was the moment she had decided to start living again. And Seb wanted to erase all that and place the blame on her? Nuh-uh.

"I almost died, Seb. I was sleeping twenty hours a day. The only thing I cared about was praying that our baby would be okay. You're right about one thing, though. When I was finally well enough to leave the hospital, I didn't question the fact that you had given up on our marriage. You made your feelings apparent the day of the accident. You didn't do a single thing that a husband ought to do when his wife is hovering between life and death. You didn't alter your plans in one single way."

Seb ran his hand through his hair. "I stayed with you until you were out of surgery. And as I told you before, I did try to extend my leave. But my CO turned me down. I talked to your dad about it, and he told me that I needed to return to base. He said he'd explain everything to you when you got out of the recovery room. I guess he kind of forgot about that."

Tacy slid down from the truck's gate and stood in front of him.

"He didn't forget. He told me your leave had run out and that you'd gone back to Texas. And then he promised that he'd do everything in his power to make sure me and the baby would be okay." She blinked back tears. She didn't quite understand why her father had behaved as he did. But she knew that he had been desperate to get her to a place best equipped to facilitate her recovery. The rehab clinic in Colorado was one of the most prestigious in the nation. And once they arrived, he had arranged for her to see a team of specialists and found a place for them to live. Drove her to the obstetrician. Bought diapers and a crib. Worked two jobs to support them and stayed with her through her long labor giving birth to Timmy.

But why had he led her to believe that Seb had been the one who wanted the divorce?

Seb bent his right leg against the side of his truck. Ten more minutes. That was how long his mom claimed she needed before she'd be ready to go. He wasn't sure if the same was true for Tacy. After their argument, she'd disappeared into the bunkhouse to look for a water bottle for Timmy. He didn't mind waiting. He welcomed the chance to think.

Why had he felt the need to reopen the subject of his possible move to Washington, DC? He knew why. Because he wanted Tacy to tell him that she didn't want him to go. That they might have a future together in Chimney Bluff as a family. But she'd never say that. She didn't want to move to North Dakota. And even if she did, she'd never forgive him for a decision he had made ten years in the past.

Of course, she still didn't know the whole story of what had happened after the accident. Yes, he had gone back to Texas, but Tacy remained in the dark about his confrontation with Keith at the hospital. Her father had heaped guilt and shame onto his shoulders with biting words that were permanently seared onto his brain. Selfish. Single-minded. Thoughtless. The last accusation had been more on point than the older man realized. Keith didn't know that Seb had stood by without protest when Tacy insisted on making the difficult climb.

Seb carried so much pain in his heart for what had happened that day on the cliffs. But it still burned to hear Tacy blame him for everything and ignore the role her father had played. Through either stubbornness or pride, she had allowed herself to be manipulated by her father and to shut everyone else out.

He had always imagined that talking things out would give him closure. But the more time he and Tacy spent discussing the past, the more confused he became. Was Tacy as indifferent as she appeared to be? It was true that he had given up after his letters had gone unanswered and his calls were not returned. But communication was a two-way street, and Tacy had never bothered to reach out to him in any way. Maybe he had done the bare minimum to save his marriage, but Tacy had done nothing at all.

Still, it had been a shock to hear how ill she had been in the months following the accident—how discarded she'd felt by him. The thought of Tacy lying in the hospital, not knowing where he was or why he left, physically hurt in his chest. He had only ever wanted to protect her. And yet she believed that he had abandoned her at the first sign of trouble. A new sense of guilt began to surge in his body, but he tamped it down. Neither he nor Tacy was entirely blameless in the events following the accident. But as he saw it, the heaviest of the fault fell squarely on one person. Keith Tolbert.

And as much as Seb hated to admit it, maybe running away to get married had been their biggest mistake. As Keith pointed out in scathing detail, if Tacy had wanted to get hitched and move to Texas, why had she applied for so many scholarships at colleges she never planned to attend? It was a good question. Some part of her must have wanted the chance to achieve the goals she had worked so hard for all of her life. And look what happened once she was free. College graduation. Law school. Success at every turn.

He took a steadying breath and twisted his head to release some of the tension knotting his neck. He wasn't going to waste any more time trying to understand Tacy's mindset. It was bad enough that Keith had deceived Tacy about the divorce, but there was no justification for his actions in keeping him from his son.

Still, there was one positive result from the whole sad series of mistakes, and that was Timmy. He and Tacy needed to get along, if only for the sake of their son.

Seb leaned against his truck and pushed his Stetson back on his head.

He was checking the weather app on his phone when his dad appeared, hauling yet another cooler toward the back of the truck. Seb hurried to help him. Five minutes later, everything was loaded, and they were ready to go. Especially Timmy, who maintained a steady stream of chatter during the drive to the church.

In the field behind the sanctuary, setup was underway. Red-and-white-checkered tablecloths flapped in the wind as a group of teens in light blue T-shirts rushed to weigh them down with rocks gathered from shore of the lake.

By two o'clock, the grills were smoking and the tables were covered with sides and desserts. An unexpected break in the clouds revealed a streak of blue and a fringe of sunshine against the gray. Seb walked over to join Tacy in cheering on Timmy in the relay race.

The strain of their previous conversation lingered in Tacy's eyes. "Awesome, considering it's his first time."

"Great. Listen. Are you still planning to enter the kayak race after lunch? Because, considering everything that's happened, you should…"

She fixed him with a resolute stare. "I'm in the orange kayak, number five. I think it belongs to one of the organizers of the picnic. I'll be fine. It's not a big deal. I've kayaked most of the lakes in Denver."

He was about to point out that his issue wasn't with her skills when the clang of the dinner bell put an end to the debate. Timmy's eyes lit up as they took their place in the food line. The tables were laden with platters of watermelon, potato salad, hot dogs and hamburgers. And every kind of cake and pie under the sun. After everyone was finished eating, an announcement was made that the kayak race would start in five minutes. Tacy pushed herself up from the table.

Seb stood. "Need some help?"

"Nope. See you at the finish line." She turned and gave him an A-OK salute.

Timmy waited until his mom was halfway down to the lake and then tugged Seb's sleeve. "Do you think Mom will win?"

"She might." The orange kayak was already in the water. All that was left for Tacy to do was clip the straps on her life jacket, grab her paddle and climb inside. He released a long sigh. He'd be glad when the race was over, and Tacy was safely back on shore.

A buzzer blared, and the race began. "And they're off," someone shouted from a table nearby. In a flurry of frothy spray, a host of kayaks launched from the shore. He felt someone brush against him, and he turned to see his mom by his side.

Timmy jumped up and down. "Go, Mom. You can do it."

It was difficult to see much from shore, but Tacy's kayak appeared to be out in front of the pack. She made a tight turn at the other side of the lake, widening her lead by at least twenty yards. With less than two miles to go, she seemed on track for an easy victory.

Seb stepped closer to the lake for a better view.

But as the racers passed the marker for the final stretch, the rain began to fall. And what started off as light drizzle quickly became a downpour. There was a flurry among the bystanders as everyone grabbed a dish and ran toward the shelter.

Seb turned toward his mom, who was standing next to Timmy. "Go on into the hall before you both get drenched. I'll come find you as soon as Tacy gets to shore."

His mom slung an arm over Timmy's shoulders. "Race you inside." With that, she took off running. He watched them for a minute and then turned his attention back to the race. It was raining harder now, and it was almost impossible to see what was happening on the lake. Heavy brown-and-green-hued clouds hung low in sky, fringed purple around the edges. He crooked his hand over his eye and squinted, searching for a slash of orange on the choppy gray.

But he couldn't see anything.

FIFTEEN

Bullet-shaped drops of rain pummeled Tacy's arms and legs as she spun her paddle through the swells. She was soaking wet, but it didn't matter. Victory was less than a hundred strokes away. Her nearest competitor, a tall, blonde woman with a red bandana tied around her hair, was twenty yards behind her. At least she was the last time Tacy checked.

Competitive juices burned through her veins. But it was becoming more difficult to stay the course as the bow of the kayak pitched forward into the foam. Waves of grey water sloshed across the hull. She adjusted her position to compensate for the chop, bracing her legs in the cockpit and holding her paddle horizontal to the deck. That should have done the trick, but it didn't. The kayak rolled to the right, tipping her sideways into the lake.

She hit the water hard but quickly broke through to the surface, twisting around to see the location of the others in the race. But the rain was falling so hard that she couldn't see anything, not even the shore.

Maybe I can still win. She flipped the kayak over and, positioning her hands on the rim of the cockpit, took a deep breath and prepared to heave herself inside. It was a move she had accomplished many times in the past, but never in these kinds of circumstances.

But as she pulled herself up, something tugged down on her leg. She pushed back against the pressure, but she couldn't break free. Had her toes gotten tangled in a clump of pondweed? She peered through the murky water as a black shadow passed beneath her.

A scuba diver? Here? At the end of the race?

The dark figure gripped her ankles and pulled again. Tacy reached around and grasped the side of the kayak, desperation welling up in her veins. Queasiness overtook her. The tug-of-war continued as she was dragged down to the bottom of the lake. Panic surged through her body as her lungs locked, desperate for air.

Three minutes. That's how long a person could survive without oxygen. How long had she been under water? One minute? Maybe two?

Long fingers scrabbled their way up her legs. Tacy pulled her knees toward her chest and pushed back hard with all her might. Pain ripped across her muscles, but she didn't stop fighting until she had kicked her legs free. She broke through to the surface, gasping for air. She filled her lungs with as much as she could take in. Even the rain, pelting against her face, felt like vindication as she raised her eyes to the sky and…

No! Those fingers were back around her ankles, relentlessly yanking her down once more. Air burbled through her mouth and her nostrils. Her stomach clenched, and her tongue tasted the bile in her throat. Timmy's sweet face flashed across her brain as she launched a sharp kick against her aggressor's shoulder. Her rib cage throbbed from the water's pressure, and her lungs felt ready to explode. But her foot made contact, and once again, she bobbed to the surface. But this time, she didn't wait. She took off like a rocket, pumping her arms, her strokes long and quick as she clawed through the waves. Her legs pounded the water with a flutter kick that was one part skill and two parts desperation. She couldn't allow herself to be pulled to the bottom again. She would make it to shore and survive.

Twelve, thirteen, fourteen. Raindrops pelted her shoulders as she counted the strokes in her head. *Twenty-one, twenty-two, twenty-three.* Exhaustion ripped through her muscles. And her lungs continued to scream for air—the short breaths she took between strokes weren't nearly enough. *Thirty-three. Thirty-four.* Her hand smashed against a solid bottom of dirt and pebbles, and before her brain could even register what was happening, she was crawling out of the water, into Seb's waiting arms.

A coil of fear tightened across Seb's shoulders as he carried Tacy toward the shore. He knew that the best response was to stay calm. But Tacy had almost drowned out there on the lake. He had almost lost her again.

"You can put me down now, Seb," she said, slipping out of his arms and collapsing into one of the chairs inside the church office. Long strands of her wet hair stuck to her face, and her clothing was soaked all the way through, dripping onto the floor.

He handed her a box of tissues that was on top of the credenza, and she pinched out a pile to wipe her face.

"Where's Timmy?" she said.

"He's in the hall playing bingo. I don't think anyone could see what was going on out there on the lake, not even the other women in the race."

"I guess I came in last," she said.

"Actually, two kayaks were still out when you

crossed the finish line. But you were probably disqualified because your kayak flipped and you swam to shore."

"No, Seb." Tears rolled down her cheeks. "My kayak didn't just overturn. Someone in scuba gear pushed it over and then tried to pull me down. It was horrible. I thought I'd never get away."

What? "I thought your kayak got knocked over in the waves."

"No," she said. Her eyes were blank as she shook her head. "Someone tried to kill me. Again."

How could he have been so oblivious? He should have known better. "Did you recognize the diver?"

"No. The water was way too murky. And when I reached the surface, it was raining so hard I could barely see two feet in front of me."

There was a knock at the door. Steven and his dad stuck their heads into the room.

"The bingo game's almost over," Steven explained. "And Timmy's wondering what happened with the race."

Tacy pulled herself up. "Thanks, Steven. I'll go talk to him and give your mom a break."

Seb made a move to follow her, but Steven stopped him. "Can I speak to you for minute? It's important," he said.

"You two go ahead and talk while Tacy and I head to the hall," his father said. "Come on, Tacy. We'll get you some towels so you can dry off and then see what's happening in the bingo game."

Seb waited until they were gone before he turned to his brother. "I want to hear your news, but I need to give you a heads-up on what just happened on the lake. Someone tried to drown Tacy during the race."

"Should I call the sheriff and have him meet us here at the church?"

Seb shook his head. "At this point, it might be best to go home and call it in from there. The way this rain is coming down, it seems unlikely that any trace of evidence remains. What did you want to tell me?"

"You're not going to believe it." Steven moved toward the door and pushed it closed. "This morning, I retraced the route we took when we were riding with Timmy. I knew I could get in trouble for poking around on Tolbert property, so I left Topper tethered in the grove and headed on foot to the mine. There were boards over the entrance, but the nails came off easily, too easily, if you ask me. I went inside and poked around. And guess what I found? Signs of recent excavation. And a six-inch-wide seam of white quartz, threaded with gold."

"Are you sure it was gold?"

Steven nodded. "As sure I can be."

This was a major bombshell. As far as Seb knew, gold hadn't been found in Chimney Bluff in over a hundred years. "If what you say is true, someone stands to make a pretty big profit when they buy Tolbert's land. I'd be surprised if Carl knows anything about this. But I'd venture to say that Gunnar Graff does. Didn't he commission a mineral survey?"

"He did, but I don't know if was completed. Just to make sure that my eyes weren't deceiving me, I snapped a couple shots of the exposed vein. The lighting is off because it was so dark, but you can see the seam as clear as day." He pulled up the pictures on his phone and then handed it across the table.

Seb scrolled through the shots. Steven was right. The vein of gold was unmistakable.

"Wow. This is crazy."

Steven nodded. "And that's not the only interesting detail I discovered today. When I drove into the church lot, I parked next to a silver sedan that looked like the one that passed me the night of Tacy's bike accident. I've been thinking about it, trying to recall any identifying details, and I had this vague recollection that there was a Wichita State decal on the back window. It struck me at the time because I remember thinking that the driver was a long way from Kansas. So when I saw the car with the same decal, it sparked my memory. And then I noticed a streak of blue on the front bumper. Took a picture of that, too."

"We need to find out who owns that car."

"Already did. Her name is Virg Smith. I met her a couple of minutes ago. She's here at the picnic with her great-granddaughter. And here's where this whole thing gets interesting. When I asked about the scratch on her bumper, Virg said that it happened when her neighbor borrowed her car. Want to guess her neighbor's name?"

Before he could answer, his brother filled in the blanks.

"Gunnar Graff," Steven said.

SIXTEEN

Seb followed Steven through the maze of cor-
ridors that led through the church. The door to
the sanctuary was closed, and meeting rooms
on the first floor were dark and deserted. But at
the bottom of the stairs, the hall was a hive of
activity. Apron-clad volunteers bustled around
wrapping up leftovers while a team of teenag-
ers collapsed tables and stacked chairs.

Tacy was waiting on the side of the room with
Timmy and his folks. Her arms were clenched
across her chest, and her eyes were hooded with
anxiety. One of the workers must have dug into
the lost and found and come up with the light
blue track suit she was wearing. It wasn't the
most current style, but at least it was dry.

He met his mom's worried glance. He wasn't
sure how much she had been told, but it must
have been enough to stir her distress.

"Everything okay here?" he asked.

"Not really," his mom said. "Dad and I need

to take Tacy and Timmy home immediately. Tacy needs to warm up. Maybe with a hot bath and then a cup of chamomile tea. And after that…"

"That sounds like a good idea, Ma. Steven and I will carry what you need to the car, and then you can head for home." He looked around the room. "Was Gunnar Graff here today?"

His mother nodded. "He was, but he left before it started to rain. Said he had some work to do back at the office. Something about a trial starting at the end of the week."

"Why are you asking about Gunnar?" Tacy asked.

"I have a couple questions for him. Not a big deal." Tacy had already been through enough, and she had always been close to Gunnar. There was no need to upset her until he had more evidence. "Steven and I might head over to his law office to see if he's around. My mom and dad can take you and Timmy home in Steven's truck."

"Can't it wait until morning?" His mom frowned. "The roads are bound to be flooded. And they'll just get worse if you delay."

"I know, Mom. But we'll be home before you know it."

His dad gestured to Timmy. "Say, young man. Can you help me carry this heavy bag out to the truck? You take one side, and I'll take the other."

Once Timmy was out of earshot, Tacy reached over and grabbed Seb's arm. "Please come back with us. I know I never should have gone out in that kayak. Sometimes…" Her voice broke. "Sometimes I'm too stubborn for my own good."

"Maybe. But who would have expected danger to follow you to the church picnic?"

"*You*. You warned me against entering the race."

He may have advised caution, but even in his wildest imaginings, he hadn't imagined that there would be a scuba diver, lurking in the lake. He hadn't even recognized it while it was happening. "Don't let your mind go there, Tace. I'll see you at home, okay?"

And as soon as the last cooler had been loaded, he and Steven headed off to find Gunnar. But the law offices were dark when they pulled into the lot. The rain soaked through their clothing as they dashed from the truck to the door.

They knocked and waited. Rang the bell and knocked again.

"Let's try his house," Seb said.

But no one answered the door there either.

"What now?" Steven asked once they were back in the truck.

"I guess we go home." Seb struggled to control his growing frustration. The never-ending merry-go-round of assaults and dead ends was wearing him down. All he wanted to do was to head back to the ranch, wrap Tacy and Timmy in his arms, and hold them secure until all of this was over.

But as he drove by a striped awning halfway past the intersection of 8th and Main, he hit the brake and pulled to a stop. "Look!" he said to Steven, pointing out the window.

"That's Lois's shop," Steven said. "Exotic Blooms for All Occasions."

"Yeah. Did you see the trashcan?" He didn't wait to hear his brother's answer. He jumped out of the truck and dashed toward the plastic bin that was tipped on its side next to a heap of trash on the pavement.

Crouching on his knees, he snatched the item that had caught his eye as they passed the store. His fingers closed around the telltale shape of a black rubber fin. He reached into the rubble and sifted around. Seconds later, he uncovered a second fin, an aluminum tank and a wet suit.

"Looks like we found our scuba diver," Steven said. "I suppose this means that we need to have a chat with Lois, though it's unlikely that she's anywhere in the vicinity."

Seb stood upright and headed across the sidewalk toward the flower store. He peered through the frosted glass of the window. "The place looks deserted. But it wouldn't hurt to poke around and see if we can find any clues about where she's gone."

He knelt down in front of the door and pulled his keychain out of his pocket. The rain spat against his face, making it nearly impossible to see the lock, but if he could wedge the file from his Swiss Army knife into the keyhole, he might be able to open the door. He gripped the tool in his wet fingers, but it slipped from his fingers and fell into a stream of water gushing across the sidewalk. Steven made a splashing leap and grabbed it before it disappeared into the overflowing sewer grate.

Seb brushed a wet hand through his soaked hair and blinked the raindrops out of his eyes. Holding the keychain steady with his left hand, he tried again to jiggle the tool into the lock. Success! The latch clicked, and the door swished open.

The still air inside the store came as a welcome relief from the lashing rain. Even more pleasant was the aroma of vanilla mingled with the scent of the sweet alyssum plants and frangipani branches that had been set in the large urns next to the door.

Steven flipped a switch. "Power's out," he said.

"It must have just happened. It's still cool in here." Seb powered up the flashlight on his phone and traced the beam back and forth around the space. The light skimmed across a wide butcher block table brimming with succulents and landed on a maroon curtain along the rear wall.

"You see what you can find in the front, and I'll check the back."

His boots left a wet trail on the smooth terracotta tiles as he tramped across the room and swept open the curtain. A gasp stuck in his throat.

Before him was a tower of terrariums and crates. A dank odor assaulted his senses as his ears picked up the hushed rustle of movement inside.

What on earth? Signs on the sides of the cages identified the terrifying lineup by name. Scorpion. Brown Recluse Spider. Cobra. King Snake.

The hairs on his arm prickled.

Steven hurried to his side. "Whoa. I wouldn't have pegged Mrs. Tolbert as a collector of spiders and snakes. I wonder where she got all these?"

"I don't know. But it can't be a coincidence that two of the empty ones are labeled Black Widow Spider and Western Rattlesnake."

Steven blew out a long breath. "I wonder what happened to that one there." He pointed to the open door of a large empty cage.

"Black Mamba." Seb's voice shook as he read the label, and then he swept his beam across the floor.

But the world's deadliest snake was nowhere to be found.

Tacy twisted the rubber band around the stack of loose cards and scraped the green houses and red hotels into the box. Getting involved in a *Monopoly* game with Timmy, Scott and Sandy had seemed like a good idea an hour earlier, but her nerves were too tense and frayed to concentrate. She could still feel those fingers clamping into her legs and pulling her down to the bottom of the lake. A shiver ran down her spine, but she shook it off. She wished that Seb and Steven would return and that everything would be okay.

Scott set the dice down into the box. "I'm going to take a stroll around the property," he said.

"Can I come?" Timmy wanted to know.

"Not this time, skipper." He shrugged on his raincoat and headed out the door.

Sandy shot a glance at Tacy. It was hard to miss the pistol tucked into the waistband of Scott's jeans.

Why hadn't Seb checked in with an update? She glanced at her phone, but there were no missed calls or texts. She set it back down again and then picked it up. No bars. So for all she knew, he could have tried.

She peered through the wet smear on the window. The storm seemed to be increasing in intensity with the winds picking up and lashing against the trees.

A deafening thunderclap was followed by a crack of lightning splitting through the clouds. The lamp on the mantel flickered for a moment and then blinked off.

"Looks like we've lost power," Sandy said. "I tried to call Scott to tell him to bring in a couple of flashlights from the garage, but I can't get any reception on my phone."

"Me, either," Tacy said.

"This is so cool!" Timmy exclaimed. "Maybe when Steven and Seb get back, we can build a fort."

A gnawing ache throbbed in her chest. For Timmy, it was a great adventure. But the thunder booms and flashes of lightning were playing havoc with her already fraught nerves.

"I've got some old oil lamps downstairs," Sandy said. "Why don't we go see if we can find them?"

"That's a great idea." Tacy knew her voice sounded overly enthusiastic, but it would feel good to do something.

"Okay." Timmy stood up reluctantly. "But maybe I should stay here and wait for Scott to get back. Or Steven or Seb."

"No!" Tacy reacted instinctively to the idea of being separated from Timmy—but when she noticed the way her shout made him flinch, she regretted her sharp pitch and added a softer tone, "I mean, no. We need your help too."

Timmy shot her a confused look, but followed Sandy toward the stairway.

Tacy flicked her phone to flashlight mode as Sandy led the way to the unfinished basement.

"This way," Sandy directed. Along the top shelf of a wooden bookcase were four oil lamps. "Be careful." Sandy stood on her tiptoes and handed two of them down to Tacy. "We haven't used these in years, so I don't know if they're empty or full." She took the remaining lamps from the shelf, and they retraced their steps upstairs.

"There. That's better." Sandy said a few minutes later. The lamps bathed the room in a flickering light. "Now we'll wait for Scott and the boys to join us."

"I'm bored," Timmy said. "Can we play another game?"

"Not right now, Timmy." Tacy was back at the window, watching for headlights, but she forced herself to relax her shoulders as she turned to face her son. "Let's wait until the others get back. Seb loves *Monopoly*. He'll definitely want to play."

"Okay. But can I go and find Cody? He might be scared by the storm. A lot of dogs are, you know."

"Oh, Cody could be anywhere," Sandy said as another peal of thunder shook the room. "He's probably holed up in the barn."

Tacy paced across the floor. The convivial atmosphere of just moments before had evaporated as the seconds of eerie darkness stretched into minutes. She stared again out the window. Shouldn't everyone be back by now? The touch of a hand on her shoulder caused her to jump.

"You need to relax." Sandy spoke in a quiet, gentle voice. "There's nothing we can do but pray and keep calm."

Tacy nodded. "It's just taking them so long. And what about this rain? Do you think there's a chance of flash flooding?"

"That's been weighing on my mind, too. We haven't had this much precipitation in a long time, and the ground isn't going to know how to handle it. But the boys can take care of themselves. It's in their blood. The Hunts and Tolberts were the first settlers in Chimney Bluff, after all."

"Really?" Timmy piped up. "Who got here first?"

Tacy shuddered another deep sigh, grateful for Timmy's interruption. Sandy's kindness was almost too much to handle. The woman had every reason to resent her—for being a Tolbert, for breaking her son's heart, for keeping her grandson away from her for almost a decade. And yet, Sandy had never shown her anything but kindness. Sandy had to be worried about her sons out there in the raging storm, but she'd taken the time to offer comfort...or at least to try.

A gust of rain lashed against the window. The storm was getting worse. What would happen if Seb and Steven got caught by a sudden rush of high water? Tears prickled at the corners of her eyes, but she brushed them away. Crying wouldn't help the situation. And really, what was she so worried about? They probably stopped somewhere in town to wait out the worst of the storm.

"Actually, Timmy, the Tolberts and Hunts came to North Dakota together." Sandy explained. "Stanley Hunt and Isaiah Tolbert were friends in Boston back in the 1860s and decided to head out West. The story is that they set out together for California, but when they reached Chimney Bluff, they agreed they had come far enough. So they bought some land for cheap, got some cattle, and settled down right next to each other. Then, as more people moved out West, the town of Chimney Bluff started to grow up as an outpost station, and Stanley and Isaiah became wealthy from trading with all the new settlers."

Tacy felt the hint of a smile flicker on her lips as she listened to Sandy. She had heard those same tales of Stanley Hunt and Isaiah Tolbert hundreds of times growing up. It started off as a fun story, even if it didn't quite stay that way once it reached the incident that instigated the feud. Everyone had a slightly different version of what had happened, but the essential details were always the same.

"Unfortunately," Sandy continued, "the more money Stanley and Isaiah made, the more they began to argue. And one day, a boundary dispute got so out of hand that the two men vowed never to talk to each other again. Stanley sued Isaiah for two hundred dollars, which was a fortune back then. And Isaiah sued him right back for defamation of his good name."

"What does defamation mean?" Timmy asked.

"It means insulting you by lying about something you didn't do."

Tacy turned back to the window. She appreciated Sandy's discretion. Timmy didn't need to know the nitty-gritty details of the hundred-year-old feud. They weren't pretty and didn't paint either the Tolberts or the Hunts in a flattering light. There were stories of the Hunts rustling cattle from the Tolberts' herd and the Tolberts failing to come to their neighbor's aid when the Hunt barn caught on fire in the fall of 1952. In her grandfather's generation, the Hunts had refused to even acknowledge the existence of their closest neighbors. Every time it seemed that the bad blood had settled between the two families, a new incident would stir the pot. And there would a fresh onslaught of petty attacks—verbal and otherwise—and ensuing lawsuits.

Timmy wanted to hear the rest of the story. "So, what happened next?" he asked.

"Hmm? Well, ever since then, they have been feuding and suing each over various differences. Even today—oh dear," Sandy paused. "The fuel in a couple of the lamps is starting to get low. I better see if I can find some more kerosene."

"We'll help you," Timmy said.

"Thank you. Tacy, could you and Timmy check downstairs? It should be in a big red jug in the cupboard. I'll take a peek to see if I left it in the kitchen."

"No problem." Tacy turned and headed to the basement with Timmy trailing behind her.

"So, if the Hunts and Tolberts don't like each other, does that mean that Seb and Steven are our enemies?" Timmy's high voice followed her down the stairs. "They don't seem like our enemies. But maybe it's like we learned in school about spies. Are we spies?"

What was Timmy talking about? Tacy rubbed her fingers against her eyes as she trained her flashlight on the top shelf of the cupboard at the bottom of the stairs. The beam wavered, illuminating row after row of canned tomatoes and pickles, but there was no sign of a red jug. She flashed her light around the space. Maybe Sandy was mistaken, and the kerosene was in the tall, metal cabinet next to the dryer. Timmy followed behind her as she shuffled across the floor toward the back wall.

"But how were you friends with Seb when you were kids if your families were enemies? And whose ranch is bigger? The Tolberts' or the Hunts'? The Hunt ranch is huge, so it's probably bigger."

"Hmm. Maybe. I'm not sure." She turned her

back against the flow of questions and roved the beam across the open shelves. "I can't see anything resembling a red jug anywhere, can you?"

"No. But can I borrow your phone for a flashlight?"

Tacy handed him her cell and pushed up on her tiptoes for a closer look. She was glad that Timmy was taking everything in stride, but his exuberance was wearying. Her brain couldn't focus on his questions when it was using all its energy to keep from worrying about Seb or reliving the moment hands had closed over her and dragged her down into the water after the kayak tipped. It had been dark under the water, and it was dark in the basement without the overhead light. Goose bumps crawled down her skin, and a shiver tingled up her body. She took a deep gulp of air. She could hear Sandy bustling upstairs in the kitchen, and the sound of the door opening at the front of the house. Maybe Scott was back. Or Seb and Steven. Her eyes finally adjusted to the darkness, and she could see that the jug had been pushed behind a large box of detergent.

"I found it," she said. "Tim?" She turned around and focused her light on the spot where Timmy had been standing.

But he wasn't there.

"Timmy! Timmy!" she cried out as she ran

up the stairs. Her heart thudded in her chest, but she pushed down the fear that threatened to overwhelm her senses. She was overreacting. Timmy had just wandered away. He didn't understand the gravity of the situation and was probably looking for Cody or something to eat. She hurried toward the kitchen where Sandy was perched on a stool by the counter. Alone.

"Where's Timmy?" Tacy asked. Her voice shook as panic rocked her senses.

"I haven't seen him since you two went to get the fuel. But I'm sure he's around here. Timmy! Timmy!" Sandy's voice echoed in the hall.

"Timmy! Timmy!" Tacy sped back down the stairs. "Timmy! Timmy!"

She could hear Sandy calling out as she made her way toward the back of the house.

Tacy skidded through the basement, checking every corner, but Timmy wasn't there. She dashed up the steps, ignoring the pang in her ankle. Hadn't she heard the swish of someone opening the front door? Maybe Timmy had gone outside looking for Scott or Cody. Her feet skimmed across the floor, but she skidded to a stop, a scream erupting from her throat.

"Tacy! What is it? Are you okay? Is Timmy hurt?" Sandy came bustling up behind her, panting from exertion. "Oh no."

Tacy felt her knees give out, and she sank to

the floor. A shiver convulsed her body, and a wave of nausea bubbled up in her throat.

Sandy knelt down beside her.

The rain was still coming down in torrents, but the front door was wide open. And the screen door was flapping in the wind. But there was enough light to see the smear of blood and the cell phone lying on the floor.

SEVENTEEN

Gale-force winds unleashed thick sheets of rain against the windshield, pounding a thunderous rhythm through the cab. Even with the wipers cranked to full speed, Seb couldn't see more than five feet ahead of them. Next to him in the passenger seat, Steven reached across the console to wipe away the condensation, but it was a temporary fix. The glass cleared for a few seconds and then fogged back up.

Seb shot a glance at his brother. "It looks like we're in for a rough ride home. I'd feel better about all of this if we'd managed to track down Gunnar or Lois. To be honest, I'm still a bit shaken after what we just saw in the shop." He blinked away the image of those snakes and spiders...and the empty cage and the missing black mamba.

Headlights blurred across the windshield as a brown sedan appeared out of nowhere, speeding toward them in their lane.

"He's not going to stop," Steven cried out in warning.

Seb hit the brake as a wave of water crashed against the truck, rocking it toward the side of the road. He glanced over at Steven and released a long breath.

That was close. Too close.

As they passed the fence to the Tolbert ranch, Steven pointed toward the turn. "Maybe we should make a quick stop and see if anyone's around at the Tolberts'."

"Okay. It might be worth it to check, if only for Carl's sake." He turned the wheel and headed down Tolbert's driveway, his heart still hammering in his chest. He left the motor running as he ran toward the house, tucked his hand into a fist, and hammered on the door. No answer. He tried again with the same result. He ran back to the truck and climbed inside. "Seems like no one's there. We can try again tomorrow."

He edged back out onto the main road. In just a few more minutes, they'd be home.

As he pulled up in front of the ranch house, his gut churned in anticipation. The soft glow of light from the kitchen window was reassuring, but the rest of the house remained in darkness. He left Steven behind as he sprinted toward the door. Halfway down the path, his foot hit an obstacle, and he stumbled off course.

"Ugh."

What was that? He clicked on his flashlight and trained the beam downward on a familiar green parka with a hood clenched at the neck.

Dad. There was a deep gash across his father's forehead. *Please God. Let him be okay.*

"Steven!" Seb cried out. "Hurry. Dad's on the ground, and he's hurt."

His father opened his eyes. His voice came in whisper. "My gun."

Seb traced his light around the immediate area. "I don't see it." He turned to face Steven, who had come up behind him. "Let's get him inside."

They looped their arms under their father's shoulders and made their way toward the house. His mom must have spotted them coming because she met them at the door. "What happened to your father? Is he okay?"

Scott grimaced. "I'm fine, Sandy. We can talk about it when we're out of the rain."

"Where's Tacy, Mom?" Seb asked.

His mother's eyes filled with tears. "Oh sweetheart, she's looking for Timmy."

Seb's heart sank all the way down to his boots. "What happened to Timmy?"

"We were getting out the oil lamps, and he was helping. Then all of a sudden, he was gone."

* * *

Tacy circled around the back of the ranch house, the beam of her flashlight focused straight ahead. How could two people disappear into thin air? Scott had been on guard with a gun at the ready. And Timmy—a sob of desperation rocked her chest—Timmy had spent most of the last hour inches from her side.

Something moved on the side of the barn. She raced toward it, slipped and landed in a puddle. She pulled herself up and sprinted forward, her breath coming out in ragged gasps.

A voice penetrated the darkness. Someone was calling her name.

"Tacy." Seb ran toward her. "Mom told me what happened. I came to help look for Timmy."

"I thought I saw him by the barn." She bent over, gasping, her body wracked by tears. "But I was wrong. There was no one there."

"It's okay."

"It's not okay. Someone took him. The screen door was open, and there was blood on the floor."

His strong arms encircled her shoulders and guided her across the yard. Inside the house, the power was still out, but the oil lamps provided enough light for her to see. Scott was sitting at the kitchen table and Sandy stood next to him, holding a piece of gauze to his head.

Tacy's hands began to shake. "Oh, no," she said.

"I'm fine," Scott growled. "Just mad. Mostly at myself. The rain was so loud that I didn't hear the person who snuck up behind me until it was too late. The worst part is that whoever hit me took my gun."

Tacy choked back a sob. "We need to find Timmy. Now."

"Before anyone goes anywhere, use these to dry off. You won't do anyone any good if you catch a chill." Sandy pointed to pile of towels she had stacked on a chair. She draped the biggest one, a large red terry cloth sheet, around Tacy's shoulders and leaned in to whisper in her ear. "We'll find him. Rest for a minute. Don't you fret."

"Thanks, Sandy." Tacy nodded. But she had no intention of staying put for longer than a minute while Timmy was somewhere outside in the rain.

Steven came into the kitchen carrying a radio. "Times like this, I'm glad there are things that still work on batteries." He fiddled with the dial until he got reception.

Brrrrrrppppp. Brrrrpppp. Brrrrrrpppp.

"The National Weather Service has issued a severe thunderstorm warning for central Billings and western Stark Counties until ten forty-five p.m. Reports of large hail and winds in excess of forty miles per hour…"

Seb checked his watch and shook his head. "I don't think we have the option of waiting this out. We need to find the sheriff and report Timmy as missing." He pulled out his keys. "Tace? You want to come with me?"

"I do," she said. She slipped the towel off her shoulders and headed for the door. A rush of wind and rain lashed against her face as she ran across the driveway and climbed into the truck. A streak of lightning blazed in the sky. Panic pressed down on her. "I'm really scared for Timmy, Seb."

"I know, Tace. Me, too. But we're going to find him. I promise."

"I'm worried about my grandfather, too."

"He wasn't home when Steven and I checked. But we don't need to jump to any conclusions."

She turned sideways in her seat and looked at Seb. His eyes were fixed ahead, and the set of his mouth was resolute. It seemed impossible that less than a week ago, he didn't even know that he had a son. But as soon as he found out, he was all in. It wasn't often that she felt an urge to open her heart, but this was one of those rare moments. Right now, before everything else got in the way, she needed to tell Seb that she was sorry—for everything.

"Seb. And all that stuff I said before when we argued about you moving to DC? I want you to know that we'll make things work, no matter where you decide to live."

He shook his head. "It's okay, Tace. I've already decided to turn down the job with the FBI."

Her eyes filled with tears. She was tired of pretending that she didn't care.

"I'm glad. I just hope you can forgive me for waiting so long to tell you about Timmy."

There. She had said it. She had put aside her fears and opened her heart. It must have been the right thing to say because Seb reached over and took her hand. Their fingers touched for only a minute, but it was enough to show that he had forgiven her.

There didn't seem much need to say more after that. Especially since their minds and hearts were focused on finding Timmy.

The sheriff's office was in chaos from the storm. With all of the accidents and stranded motorists on the roads, resources were stretched thin, and only a skeleton staff remained behind to manage the radios. The sheriff himself had been called out to deal with a rollover involving multiple fatalities and a semi jackknifed across the road. But the kidnapping of a child took immediate precedence. The desk clerk ushered them into a small room, where the deputy in charge was quick to respond. They were assured that all available personnel would be mobilized immediately. An Amber Alert was issued. The FBI was notified, and so were the police in Bismarck and Fargo and Grand Forks.

The deputy glanced up from the paperwork scattered over her desk. "Do either of you have a picture of Timothy? Maybe on your phone or in your wallet?"

Tacy reached into her purse to pull out her phone, but Seb beat her to it. "I took this the other day when we were playing baseball."

The deputy nodded. "I'll make a copy, and we'll get it out on the wire."

Tacy slid her own phone across the desk. "Timmy was using my cell as a flashlight when he was abducted. I found it by the front door. Maybe you can pull some prints."

The deputy opened the desk drawer and took out a plastic bag. "We'll check on that and get your phone back so you'll have it in case the kidnapper calls. Our mobile task force will be out to the ranch to monitor all your devices as soon as the towers come back up. In the meantime, we're going to stay on this, checking the wire and monitoring any information coming in from federal and local agencies."

The deputy was true to her word. A quarter

of an hour later, they had their phones back and were headed through the empty corridor leading out of the station.

"Wait." An authoritative voice halted them in their tracks. They turned to see the deputy rushing to stop them at the door.

"We just had a report of yet another multi-car crash," she said. "It might make sense to wait the storm out here."

Seb shook his head. "I appreciate the advice, but we need to get home."

"Okay. But take it slow and easy." She turned and disappeared into a room in the middle of the hall.

Tacy took a deep breath and pushed back tears. "I'm scared, Seb. What if no one calls? What if this isn't a kidnapping? What if…"

"Tacy, stop. Someone will call."

She shook her head. She could only pray.

EIGHTEEN

Back at the ranch, everyone was still in the kitchen, listening to the radio. Sandy stood up to meet them at the door. "What did the sheriff say about Timmy?"

Tacy shook her head. A wave of hopelessness washed over her. There was nothing positive to report. The kidnapper was still out there. The phone lines were still down. And her baby was still missing.

Scott took one look at their faces and stood up. "It's getting late. Let's all try to get some sleep." After a brief discussion, it was agreed that Tacy should take Seb's bedroom. Seb had insisted on staying on the main floor to keep watch, and she didn't have the energy to argue. Her body felt drained and her head foggy.

Her face must have reflected her distress because Scott clapped an arm around her shoulder, giving a kind squeeze. "I know this is tough, but things will look better in the morning."

Could that be true? Probably not, but there was nothing to do but trudge up the stairs, leaving Seb behind, tucking a fresh sheet around the corners of the couch.

Slowly and carefully, she went through the motions of preparing for bed. Washed her face and brushed her teeth. Plumped the pillows and turned down the quilt on the bed. But all she could think about was Timmy. Was he hurt? Was he frightened? She stretched out and tried to sleep. Twisted and turned. Flipped onto her back and pushed her sweat-soaked hair off her forehead as an icy fear seeped through her veins. What if her son was dead?

She pounded her fists against the mattress. She had no tears left to cry. All that remained was a paralyzing anxiety. And anger at herself for letting her guard down and allowing Timmy to wander from her sight.

The whole evening had been a colossal exercise in frustration. Maybe Scott was right. Maybe everything would sort itself out in the morning—but that sure seemed hard to believe.

The morning. When did that officially begin, anyway?

She looked at the time on her old clock on the nightstand. 3:07. Still too early to get up and go downstairs. She flipped back over onto her stomach, closed her eyes and forced her body to relax. Slowly, she drifted off.

Buzzzzzzzzzzzzzz. Buzzzzzzzzzzzzzz.

Her body jerked upright. Was that her cell? The towers must be back up and working if someone had sent her a text.

She needed to tell Seb about the phones immediately. But…wait. Her eyes were drawn to the words piling up in neat columns on the screen.

For your eyes only.

Your grandfather has gold coins hidden at the ranch. Find them.

If you want to see your son again, bring them to the ledge on Shepherd's Peak.

Come alone.

Tacy scrolled back up and reread the texts. Gold coins in exchange for Timmy. She could do that. The harder part to swallow was that the person had told her to come alone. She longed to talk to Seb to see what he thought. But that might anger the kidnapper and put Timmy in danger. And Seb might tell her not to go, or insist that they wait to consult with the sheriff.

Who knew how long that could take? She took a breath and made a decision.

If Seb was awake when she came down the stairs, she'd show him the text. But if he was asleep, she'd handle it herself.

She grabbed her shoes, slipped on her jeans and sweatshirt and crept down the steps. Seb was curled up on his side, facing the back of the couch. He didn't move as she walked by him toward the kitchen. Well, that settled that. The keys to his truck were on the counter by the stove. She snagged them and slipped out the door.

The rain had finally stopped, but mud sloshed under her feet as she dashed toward the barn. If memory served her, Seb kept his climbing gear hooked along the back wall of the hayloft. She swung open the door and flicked on the overhead light. She sat down and pulled on her sneakers as her eyes adjusted to the brightness. Yes! There, propped between the riding mower and a wheelbarrow was a helmet, a set of ropes, and a plastic bag full of carabiners.

She stuffed everything into a backpack, and, a minute later, she was on the road. The beams of her headlights illuminated a rain-slicked tarmac covered with fallen branches and puddles full of water from the storm.

Should she have left Seb a note to tell him

where she was going? Probably. Her fingers clenched the steering wheel. But if she'd left a note, Seb might come after her, and the text had said to come alone. She wasn't about to take any chances with Timmy's life.

Was Lois the kidnapper? The answer to that question kept changing in her brain. Wouldn't Lois know how to access her grandfather's stash of gold? But if not Lois, who else could it be?

The ranch house was dark as she pulled into the driveway. She slipped her key out of her pocket and unlocked the door, trying to calculate the most likely place to find the coins.

She let the beam of her flashlight rove through the small storage space under the stairs. It had been her favorite hiding place when she was a kid, but it seemed unlikely that anything valuable would be hidden in there. She bent down and peered inside. Just as she thought. Nothing but cobwebs and dust. A memory popped into her brain. She had been about ten when she had come into the kitchen to see her grandfather dropping coins into an old coffee can. He'd winked at her and offered some sage advice. "If there's something you want to keep secret, hide it in plain sight."

In plain sight. She walked into the kitchen and looked around. She began opening cabinets, but there was nothing inside but everyday dishes and glassware, stacked neatly on the shelves. What about the pantry? She let her gaze scrape over the cereal boxes and rows of canned vegetables. After a moment, her eyes lit upon the bent edge of an oversized can at the back of the bottom shelf. She pushed aside a couple of jars of sweet pickles, and there it was. The very same can she had seen her grandfather holding in the kitchen all those years ago. It was heavy. And it jangled when she picked it up. She was about to pry open the top when the clip-clopping of boots against the kitchen floor alerted her that someone had come into the room.

Could it be her grandfather? Seb had checked earlier and said he hadn't been home. But what if Seb was wrong—or her grandfather had arrived back in the hours since then? Or maybe it was Lois. Her eyes darted to the left and to the right. There wasn't anywhere to hide. The footsteps were getting closer. Tension rose like a fever in her heart.

Click. The pantry light blinked on. Her stomach churned with disappointment. Not her grandfather. She stared up at the bemused face of Len Jones.

"Tacy-girl! What are you doing here? I saw the light and assumed it was Mr. Tolbert."

Her heart was still pounding against her rib

cage as she scrambled to find words. "No. No. It's me. I came here to get something."

Len gave her a curious look. "What could be so important to bring you here this early in the morning? I heard you were staying at the Hunts. Is everything okay?"

"Yeah." She tried to hide the shaking in her voice as his eyes zeroed in on the battered can she was clutching in her arms.

"What'll you be wanting with that old thing?" Len asked.

"Nothing, really. I just need to take it with me. Trust me, okay?"

"Well, sure I trust you. You being a Tolbert and all. But maybe we should let someone know that…"

Her cell vibrated in her pocket, and she checked the screen. Her breath hitched. Another text.

She turned away from Len to read it. But there was nothing to read. It was just a map of Shepherd's Peak with an X on the ledge near the top.

Len moved beside her. "Are you sure there's nothing I can do to help? I know my way around these parts like the back of my hand." He gave her a shrewd look.

An overwhelming desire to take him up on

his offer crashed down on her, but she squared her shoulders and shook her head.

No one could help her. The message had said she needed to come alone.

"I appreciate it, Len. But no. I've got to leave now. But thanks for watching the house and for everything."

She pulled the can against her chest and backed out of the pantry. It was heavier than she expected, and her fingers itched to look inside. But she didn't want to raise Len's suspicions any more than she already had. She could feel his eyes on her as she walked toward the truck.

Slipping the key in the ignition, she gave a quick wave as she backed down the driveway and turned onto the main road.

She drove for five minutes before pulling over. What if the can was filled with rusty old nails? Even though she was in a hurry, she had to stop and make sure. She pried the lid off and stared down at a glittering pile of loose coins. She picked one up and weighed it in her hand. It felt cold and substantial. Didn't people in movies and books always check to see if the gold was real by biting it? She brought the coin to her lips and bit down. It was surprisingly supple. She tossed it back into the can and pushed down on the lid, and then she merged back onto the road.

It was a thirty-minute drive to Shepherd's Peak, but if she kept a heavy foot on the accelerator, she could make it in under twenty. Threads of light were already beginning to show in the eastern sky as the speedometer hovered at seventy.

She approached the final turn to the cliffs, still wavering about which way to go. If she chose the quicker route around the front of the rocky outcropping, she'd need to climb to reach the ledge. Could she do so encumbered with a backpack full of extra weight? The memory of what had happened ten years ago still filled her with dread.

The second option, the easier option, was to take the path along the back of the plateau. But the narrow trail had been designed for ATVs. She'd never reach the top in Seb's truck, and going on foot would slow her down tremendously.

She tightened her grip on the wheel and pushed the speed up to seventy-five.

Dread washed over her. She was going to have to climb.

Seb didn't expect to fall asleep folded up like a taco on the living room couch. But he must have dozed off, at least for a while, because when he looked at his phone, the time flashed five a.m.

Wait. He rubbed the grit from his eyes. Forget the time. His cell had four bars. The towers must be up. That was just the jolt of adrenaline he needed to power him awake.

He headed into the kitchen and flicked on the light. Great. Now they were in business. The power was back, too.

Cody looked up from his bed and yawned in greeting.

"Hey, boy," He said, ruffling the pup's furry head. "Looks like it's going to be just you and me for a while."

He dropped a dark roast pod into the Keurig and leaned against the counter to watch the machine hiss and puff out six ounces of strong java. He took his cup over to the table and sipped. Now that the cell towers were back up, it wouldn't be long before the FBI arrived to set up their equipment to monitor the phones. Plus, a glance out the window showed that the rain had stopped, which meant the search for Timmy could begin in earnest.

But he had no intention of sitting around and waiting for the kidnapper to make contact when he could be figuring out where Lois or Gunnar had stashed Timmy.

Cody's wet nose pressed against his hand,

and the pup's liquid brown eyes looked up at him beseechingly.

"You're ready for your chow?"

Cody thumped his tail and nudged next to him as he walked to the cupboard and measured out a cup of dried food and poured it into the bowl. Hard to believe a pup could be that desperate for breakfast.

His eagerness reminded him of Timmy. He paced across the kitchen, the need to be proactive itching across his brain. If nothing else, he could re-review his notes on the case. But his computer was on his desk in the room where Tacy was sleeping. He decided to take the risk and see if he could creep in and retrieve it without waking her up. He tiptoed up the stairs and slowly turned the knob.

What? His eyes blinked in disbelief. The bed was empty, and there was a pile of rumpled sheets on the floor. His heartbeat quickened. Where was Tacy? He tried for calming breaths. There was probably a good reason why she wasn't in bed. She was probably right around the corner or somewhere down the hall.

But no. He rushed toward the bathroom, but she wasn't inside. And the upstairs porch was dark and empty. Trepidation hastened his footsteps as he ran down the stairs to check the driveway. His truck was gone. And a set of footprints in the mud led into the barn and toward the back wall where he kept his climbing gear.

The hooks were empty. What? Why?

His heart pounded. Tacy would never attempt a climb in her current state of exhaustion. Unless…

A tinge of unease spread across his chest. Unless she thought it was the only way she could rescue Timmy.

Maybe—he could only hope—she had left a message on his cell. He looked down at his phone and saw a missed call.

But it wasn't from Tacy. It was from Len Jones.

Why would the Tolberts' ranch hand be trying to reach him at four thirty in the morning? He hit the return button, and waited for Len to answer.

"Hey, this is Seb Hunt. You wanted to talk to me?"

"Sure thing, Seb." Len's tone was slow and easy. As if he had all the time in the world. "Tacy came by here a while ago and was poking around the kitchen. She seemed pretty upset. I've always had the impression that the two of you had a bit of history, so I thought you might like to know."

"Do you know what she was looking for?"

"I'm not rightly sure. But she was hanging on to an old coffee can, and she seemed to be in an awful hurry."

"Did she say where she was going?"

"Nah," Len said. "But I happened to glance over at her phone, and I saw a map of Shepherd's Peak."

Shepherd's Peak. Dread swamped his senses. In the almost seven weeks he had been home, he had been careful to avoid that particular place. Too many bad memories. Too many broken dreams.

Surely Tacy wouldn't be so foolhardy as to venture a climb to its peak. The ascent was difficult in the best of circumstances, but add in the recent deluge of water, and the rocks would be slippery and the ground muddy.

But even as his brain marshalled these thoughts, his heart knew the truth. Of course, Tacy would attempt the climb if she thought she could rescue Timmy. He would do the same.

He pivoted on his heel and dashed back into the house. His truck was gone, so he grabbed nearest keys. Thirty seconds later, he shot down the driveway, his body hunched down low against the handlebars of Steven's motorcycle. The needle on the speedometer edged toward seventy, but he continued to press down on the accelerator. He had to get to Shepherd's Peak. He had to save Tacy and Timmy.

NINETEEN

By the time Tacy parked next to the rock-strewn path to Shepherd's Peak, the sun was already peeking up from the horizon, and a thick mantle of humidity hung in the air. A bead of sweat trickled down her back, but she squared her shoulders and quickened her pace. Her eyes scanned the sides of the cliff and stopped to focus on the ledge. Was Timmy up there, waiting? She'd find out soon enough.

She took a step. Then another. She could this. She had to do this.

But after twenty minutes, her ankle was throbbing, and a stabbing pain jolted up her body with each step. The coffee canister inside her backpack jangled, its rounded edges rubbing against her spine, and the canvas straps chafed against her shoulder blades. Sweat soaked through her shirt, and her hair was damp with perspiration. But none of that mattered. She needed to rescue Timmy.

Timmy with his dark, thoughtful eyes. His straight brown hair that was so like Seb's. The freckles that sprinkled his nose. And his smile. His perfect smile that would light up his whole face with excitement and eagerness. Images of her son throughout the years flashed in her mind. Timmy as a baby. He had been so small and frail. The doctor had induced her a month early when her infection left her too weakened to carry him full-term. But Timmy had strength. From the very first moment he was born at just under five pounds, he hadn't let his small body hold him back. He had cried gustily for milk and seemed to have set his mind on living. Then there was Timmy at his first birthday, just beginning to walk. Her father had bought him new gray Nike sneakers that matched his own, and Timmy had proudly staggered around their two-bedroom apartment with her dad following in case he fell.

Oh Dad. She sniffled back tears. *Why did you ask me to come back here? Why didn't you reach out to Grandfather before you died to tell him whatever it was that you wrote in your letter?* Not that the letter even seemed important anymore, not with Timmy somewhere on the cliffs. It was a good thing that Seb now knew that he had a son. If anything happened to her, Timmy would still have a family to love.

She wiped her eyes on the shoulder of her shirt and began to mentally prepare for the challenge ahead. *Please God. Give me strength.*

As she crested the steeper part of the mountain, her phone pinged with a text. She glanced down at the screen. It was a report on the drug test done by the clinic. High levels of sedatives had registered in her saliva.

So Lois had drugged her coffee, not that it mattered at this point. She paused to catch her breath. In another hundred feet she would be below the ledge.

And then she would have to climb.

Her overheated body was suddenly blanketed with an icy chill. No! She was not going to have another panic attack. Not here. Not now. She sat down on a rock and lowered her head between her knees, forcing herself to relax, to inhale and exhale slowly. After ten seconds, her heart rate returned to normal, and she stood up. It didn't matter what had happened before. Today she was going to make it to the ledge.

She trudged on. The cliff loomed closer and closer. And then, suddenly, she was there. At the end of the trail. Staring up at the rock wall in front of her. Scrubby bits of brush grew along the side, and the tan stone looked almost yellow in the sunshine. She brushed a hand across her face and looked around. It was just as she remembered. Her eyes skimmed over the edifice toward the narrow crevice two thirds of the way up. That was the spot where she had fallen while climbing with Seb.

She stared at the wall and took a deep breath. This time she would do it right. If her accident had taught her one thing, it was not to rush— no matter how desperately she wanted to. She hung the rope across her shoulder and placed the safety helmet on her head. There was no doubt left lingering in her mind. She was going to nail the climb and save Timmy.

Clumps of goopy gravel clung to the front wheel of the Harley, miring it down in a sinkhole of sludge. Seb gunned the bike's engine, but it didn't do any good. The tires spun uselessly in the mud. He should have realized that the ground was too wet from the rain. He took a deep breath and slid off the motorcycle. He'd go the rest of the way on foot. But he needed to hurry. Judging from the fresh ATV tracks carved into the wet ground, someone had already passed by ahead of him. Lois? Maybe. Or maybe Gunnar. Definitely not Tacy unless she had abandoned his truck for a lighter vehicle.

He was tempted to text her and let her know that he was halfway up the back trail of Shepherd's Peak. But it would be a risky move without any sort of knowledge of her whereabouts. He began to sprint and then eased into a jog as the path became steeper and pockmarked with rocks. One step up and two steps back.

A sudden realization flashed across his brain. He had spent the past ten years mourning the loss of something that was within his reach— but he had lacked the courage to go for it. When this was all over, when Tacy and Timmy were safe, he'd ask for a chance to make new start. But first he needed to deal with the kidnapper.

He increased his pace as the path leveled off, but despite the easier terrain, it was difficult to gain traction. His boots slid at every foothold, and his lungs burned with each ragged breath. But just another fifty yards and he'd be there.

As he made the final push to the top, he locked in on a plan of attack. The kidnapper had probably heard the motorcycle before he had abandoned it on the path, so it seemed likely that he or she would be ready and waiting. And, even though the kidnapper probably had his dad's gun, Seb was armed as well. The wild card in the situation was going to be Timmy. Would he be there on the ledge, or had he been left behind in a safe place? Seb was praying it would be the latter. This would be a lot easier if he didn't have to worry about Timmy.

Ten feet to go. Then five. His heart was

pounding when he reached the plateau at the top of the cliff where an ATV was parked off to the side.

Adrenaline coursed through his body as he drew his weapon and he stepped up on the summit. His breath hitched as he looked down at the person waiting for Tacy.

Gunnar Graff.

There was no sign of Lois. Part of him still wondered what role she played in all of this. Had she and Gunnar been working together all along? Who had formulated the plan? Who was it who kept raising the stakes? Seb couldn't know for sure—and now wasn't the time to find out.

A flash of color caught his eye. At his feet was a red carabiner attached to a rope dangling down to the ledge. A couple inches to the right, propped against the back wall, was a small wooden crate. And next to that crate was Timmy.

Fury raged through his senses. He clicked off the safety from his gun and was lining up his shot when the scuffing of boots echoed against the rocks. He looked toward the sheer side of the outcropping. Ten fingers grasped the ground inches from where Gunnar was standing. Then, Tacy—her long hair tucked into his red helmet and her cheeks streaked with mud and dirt—pulled herself up onto the ledge.

"Gunnar!" Tacy's voice betrayed her dismay. "Why are you here? Where's Lois?"

Gunnar laughed. "Figured out she was involved, did you? Good—I wanted you to. That way, you'd never think to suspect me."

"Suspect my godfather? My father's best friend? No, it never occurred to me," Tacy spat back. "How could you do this? And *why*? Just for a container of gold coins? Was that worth selling out your friends?"

"Oh, there's much more to it than a container of gold," Gunnar replied with a sneer. "You have no idea how big this deal truly is."

Seb shifted in his position on the outcropping. A sharp-edged rock dug into his abdomen, but he ignored the throbbing and raised his gun. His finger twitched on the trigger, but Gunnar and Tacy were too close together. If he hit Gunnar, he might fall—and take Tacy with him.

"I had a chance to finally make a big score by setting up a dummy corporation to buy the land from your grandfather." Gunnar continued. "The land that holds an actual, literal gold mine that your grandfather never even suspected was there. If my scheme had worked, I'd never have to worry about money again."

Anger tinged with disbelief pooled in Seb's

gut. Money? This whole vendetta against Tacy was because of greed? Somehow it had seemed so much more personal. But the fact that Gunnar would throw away his decades of friendship with the Tolberts just for such material stakes didn't surprise him. He had always been wary of the attorney.

He rolled his head back against his neck. He couldn't get a shot off from his current position. But Gunnar's obsession with gaining the gold might be his undoing. A plan began forming in his brain.

As Seb considered his options, Gunnar moved a step closer to Tacy on the ledge. "But you ruined it. I knew when you came back to town that you'd bring trouble. You and your fancy law school degree. It was only a matter of time before you found out about that old deed your grandfather sent your dad years ago. I convinced your grandfather that it was never official. But I knew you'd be too smart to be fooled by my lies.

"Of course, your father didn't destroy it. Why would he, when it guaranteed your future? He told me about it just before he died. Asked me to follow through with Carl to see if a joint tenancy agreement was something he still wanted. Said he'd wait to hear from me before discussing the matter with you."

Gunnar's features hardened as he drew out the pistol he had tucked into his waistband and aimed it at Tacy's chest. "He didn't know that I had been working for years on my own plan and that helping his daughter was the least of my concern."

The hairs on the back of Seb's neck stood up at the sight of Gunnar pointing his weapon at Tacy. But there was no way he was going to let anything happen. Not to Tacy. Not to Timmy. If it was the last thing he did, he was going to save the woman he loved and the son he had just found. Or he would die trying.

"Mom!" Timmy cried out from the nest of cords binding his arms and his legs.

"Timmy!" Tacy moved toward him. But she had taken only a few steps when a bullet blazed above her in the air.

"Stay away from your son. If you move any closer, I'll kill you…and him."

Fury coursed through Seb's body. He estimated the distance to the bottom of the ledge. The ten-foot jump wouldn't be a problem, but it would only take a second for Gunnar to get a shot off, and this time he wouldn't be firing a warning shot. There would be no room for mistakes.

"Did you bring the gold?" Gunnar said.

Tacy nodded. She made a move to slip off

her backpack, but Gunnar stopped her with a bullet that skidded across the dirt. "Toss it to me. And don't try anything stupid if you care about your son."

Tacy looked toward Timmy and then glanced up toward the top of the cliff. Did she see him? She must have, because she heaved the pack across the ground directly under the spot where he was crouched and waiting.

"Stupid girl!" Gunnar yelled. "Didn't I tell you to throw it here?" He moved across the ledge, keeping the barrel of his gun fixed on Tacy. He bent down and ripped open the backpack, clawing through the contents, tossing carabiners and ropes over the cliff. He pulled out the old coffee can, yanked off the top, and reached inside.

Seb flexed his toes. That was his chance.

He jumped.

Gunnar's eyes caught on him while he was still in midair.

There was a flash of light, but Gunnar's shot went wide. Seb flinched sideways, missing his landing and crashing his left foot through the top of the cage. The wood splintered under his boot, but he shook himself free and charged.

He knocked Gunnar to the ground, and the impact sent both weapons skittering.

Tacy scrambled to reach a gun, but Seb beat

her to it. As his fingers closed around the trigger, a movement caught his eye—a long snake slithering free from the broken boards of the cage.

For one painstaking second, everyone froze.

This must be the black mamba that had been missing from Lois's shop. His already pounding heart accelerated as the snake twitched its tail and flicked his forked tongue. It didn't look that much different than a harmless grass snake. But its olive skin glistened as it zigzagged from left to right across the ledge.

Sweat dripped from his forehead as he pointed his gun at the snake. The shot would be difficult since the mamba's movements were wily—and quick. Its glistening body glided in semicircles around the rocks, its neck raised and his head cocked to one side, its black eyes surveying the scene. He had to do something. If the snake bit Timmy or Tacy…

No. That wasn't going to happen. He steadied his shaking hands and whispered a prayer.

Guide me, Lord.

He pulled the trigger and fired.

The snake recoiled as the bullet struck. It hissed and lashed forward, its jaws clamping down on Gunnar's outstretched arm.

A howl of despair burst from Gunnar's throat as the injured snake wrapped its tail around his elbow and, in a flash of fury, bit deeper through his flesh.

Gunnar stumbled backwards.

Seb reached out his hand as Gunnar teetered for a moment on the edge. But it was too late. With the snake's jaw still clamped down onto his arm, Gunnar lost his balance and fell backward off the ledge.

TWENTY

The horror was over. Timmy was safe. In the days that followed, a funnel cloud of emotions swirled through Seb's brain. Relief and gratitude. Faith and hope in God's plan for the road ahead. Respect and love for his parents and Steven, who'd had his back throughout the crisis.

But inside of him another, more complicated emotion danced in his head. Sadness. After ten years apart, he had finally found Tacy. The moment when he realized that he could lose her forever had clarified his thoughts. He had been blind and stubborn to hold on to old grudges and try to assign blame. It didn't matter what had happened with the divorce. That was part of the past, part of a time when they were both too young to realize what they had to lose. But now, ten years older and quite a bit wiser, he saw clearly what was already gone and what he could miss out on in the future. Love. A wife. A son. A family. They were all he wanted—and he was terrified he'd already missed his chance.

He and Tacy had been pulled in many different directions since arriving at the base of Shepherd's Peak. There were interviews with the police and the FBI and frantic attempts to find Carl, who turned out to be holed up in a hotel, waiting out the storm. Lois had left him there, promising to return, but the feds picked her up at the airport, boarding a plane to Montreal.

Gunnar was dead. And Lois was claiming to be a victim of blackmail. With Gunnar threatening to expose her past, she had become his accomplice in several of Tacy's accidents. But she had been adamant that the more deadly attacks had been all Gunnar, that he had set her up by planting the scuba gear in front of her shop and acted alone in the kidnapping. But she was going to have a hard time proving her case, given her deadly menagerie of reptiles and snakes.

In the short bursts of time Seb and Tacy had been able to spend together, Seb had seen deeper emotions reflected in her eyes—sadness, longing, maybe even love. She said that she wanted to leave the past behind. But was she hoping to move forward in the same ways that he was?

If only he knew for sure.

The details were still being discussed, but right now it appeared that sometime in September, Timmy would spend a week in Chimney Bluff for a trial run, as Tacy had called it. But what did that mean? He worried that if it didn't work, she might want to go back to the way it had been before he knew that he had a son.

But, no, that wasn't fair to Tacy. She had been nothing but reasonable during their talks about Timmy's future.

So, why was he focusing on worst-case scenario? Maybe because a whole passel of complications had nudged into his head. Turning down the job with the FBI had seemed like a sensible option. But now, with Timmy and Tacy leaving, the looming prospect of ranch life seemed just a bit bleak. And what about the logistics? Did they even let nine year-old kids fly by themselves these days? Probably not, which would mean Tacy would have to come along when Timmy visited.

Which could be a good thing. Or not. He didn't want to assume anything.

He blew out a sigh and shook his head. He was doing it again. He was thinking about problems rather than opportunities. Tacy was still here, at least for the moment, which meant that he still had a chance to convince her to stay.

Once upon a time, he and Tacy had something precious and wonderful. For a while, it seemed that they had lost it, but it had always been there, just out of reach. This past week had been a journey of forgiving and being forgiven. His heart drummed against his rib cage. Ten years ago, he had stood by silently and allowed himself to lose what was most important in his life. Not again. He slammed down his coffee cup and headed outside to the front of the house.

He needed to tell Tacy that he still loved her. Now. What was the worst that could happen? She'd tell him that she didn't feel the same way? His heart would be broken? It already was. At least then he wouldn't have to waste any more time wallowing in regret. Today he was going to do what he should have done a long time ago. Fight for the woman he loved.

Steven's motorcycle was parked in the middle of the driveway, keys dangling from the ignition. Seb cranked the throttle and sped out of the drive, turning at the fork toward the Tolberts' ranch.

He took a shortcut along the path between the two properties. The ground was already cracked and dry despite all the rain that had fallen during the storm. As he passed the hill by the buffalo enclosure, he blinked at the blur of color headed his way—Tacy galloping toward him on a chestnut stallion. Her loose golden hair flowed behind her just like it used to when she was a kid, and for a moment, he felt like they were their teenage selves, meeting in secret to discuss their future.

Their future. That was what lay before them now. His heart lurched. Her horse came to a stop, and Tacy dismounted and ran toward him. A bubble of hope began form in his chest.

"I thought you were spending the day with Carl and Timmy at the ranch."

She shook her head. "No. I have something to show you, and I couldn't wait. My grandfather was going through Lois's closet this morning when he was packing up some things to bring to her in jail."

"Is he doing okay?"

"As well as can be expected. He's glad that he won't have to leave the ranch. But he still seems to be in love with Lois, so it's hard to imagine what happens next. But what I came here to tell you was that he found my dad's letter in one of Lois's drawers. She must have been holding on to it as leverage over Gunnar." Tacy reached into her pocket and handed him an envelope with a broken seal. "I read it to my grandfather this morning, but I want you to read it too."

He opened the flap, taking out the note, and stared down at the two pieces of paper in his hands. The last thing he wanted to do was to get bogged down discussing Keith Tolbert. The man had exerted a tremendous influence on Tacy while he was alive. And it appeared that he was making his presence known once again, this time from the grave.

"Seb?" Tacy bent her head to one side, waiting for him to begin.

Okay. He'd do as she asked. But once he finished, he was determined to share the truth that was in his heart. That he loved her. He could only hope that she felt the same way.

She looked at him expectantly. So he read.

"'Dear Dad and Tacy,'" he began. "Wait. I thought this was meant for your grandfather."

"Just keep reading," she said. "It will all become clear very soon."

He hoped so. "'I am addressing my words to both of you since this is something you both need to hear. A confession. An unburdening from a man who wouldn't—or couldn't—admit his mistakes until he was gone. A flawed man. But a man who loved his family more than life.'"

Seb paused again. This wasn't what he had been expecting. He looked up at Tacy. Her eyes were full of tears. "Are you sure you're okay with me reading this?"

She nodded, so he continued. "'Mistakes. That's a complicated word. Sounds benign, but it's really quite the opposite. In any case, I seem to have cornered the market on messing things up. All done with good intentions, but that didn't stop my actions from being wrong. So, indulge a dying man this bit of whimsy. If I could go back to do things over, this is what I'd do...

"'One. I would have never shown such disrespect to the man who raised me and taught me about life. I was angry and upset about so many things, and I honestly believed that Tacy might die if I didn't get her to that clinic in Colorado, but that's no excuse. Dad, I know that you were just trying to offer support and help me see reason, but my heart was too closed to listen. I know I hurt you, and for that, I am so sorry. I love you, and I beg you to forgive me for shutting you out.'"

Seb brought his glance back to Tacy, who had tears running down her cheeks. "This is really personal. Are you sure you want me to keep going?"

"I'm sure," she said.

"Okay." He focused back on the letter. "'Two. And this one's for you, kiddo. Tacy-girl. Light of my life. I know you assumed that Seb left because he couldn't handle the fallout from the accident. But that wasn't true. I allowed you to think that because I believed that you needed to get on with your life, and I didn't want you to end up stuck on some army base, alone and barely able to make ends meet. You had so many colleges to choose from, dozens of scholarships, such a promising road ahead. And I was convinced that you deserved a better life than Seb could provide. That's what I told him that first day at the hospital—that he would never be able to make you happy. I took advantage of his sadness and confusion to make him feel guilty for what had happened on the cliff, and for the life you'd face with him going forward. I blamed him for ruining your life. I insisted that the honorable thing to do was to allow you some space to make your own decision.'"

Seb took a break to release a long breath. Everything Keith said was true, but he had never expected him to admit it. What had Tacy thought when she had read these words? He didn't dare venture another glance in her direction. He felt too raw. Too exposed. He focused again on the letter. There was just one more paragraph to go.

"'I said that he had coerced you into marrying him. I showed him a list of all the college acceptances you had received, and I asked him point blank why he thought you had applied to so many places if you were intending to get hitched.'"

Tacy reached over and touched his hand.

"Why didn't you tell me what my dad said at the hospital?"

He raised his head to return her glance. "I wanted to. But for a long time I believed that what he said was true. That you were better off without me and that getting married had been a mistake—or at least, that you believed it was, and that that was why you ignored all my attempts to contact you and then sent me divorce papers."

"Do you still think that?"

"No." He shook his head. "That's why I was coming to see you. To ask for a second chance. Your dad talked a lot about mistakes in his letter. Well, I made plenty of them, too. I'm so sorry that you thought I didn't care. But I'll never let anything come between us again. I love you, Tace. I think I knew that from almost from that first moment I saw you standing in the field. It took me a long time to admit my mistakes, but I promise to always be there for you and our son."

Tacy pushed back the tears. Her heart felt like it was about to explode in her chest. Seb loved her. She wanted to tell him that she loved him, too. But there was one last thing, the biggest thing that had come between them. He needed to hear the truth about the divorce. "There's one more part to the letter. On the back of the page. It explains the reasons why we spent ten years apart."

Seb took a deep breath and prepared to give voice to Keith Tolbert's final words. "'Last but not least, my greatest deceit, I lied when I told you that Seb had filed for the divorce. I was the one who initiated the paperwork, for a lot of the same reasons I stated above, but for some other, selfish ones, too. What you do with this information is up to you. As for me, I've asked for the Lord's forgiveness as well as yours, and I pray that in time you can understand and forgive me, too.'"

Seb folded the notepaper in half and handed it back to her.

She wiped her eyes on the sleeve of her shirt.

She had already reread the letter so many times, but hearing Seb speak her dad's words out loud had caused a seismic shift in her heart. The man she had kept on a pedestal for her whole life had feet of clay. He was flawed like all God's creatures, but she found that she could forgive those flaws since she knew that everything he had done had been born out of love for her, his only daughter.

But the grace of the moment was in the present, not the past. And her heart was brimming with love for the man standing before her. Seb had already lost ten years of being a father. A husband. A friend. The past didn't matter anymore. They had their entire future in front of them.

"I love you, too, Seb Hunt." She yanked on the hem of his T-shirt and pulled him toward her.

When his lips met hers, she understood what it meant to reclaim a forever love. And if that moment of clarity had to happen somewhere, why not in the middle of a pasture they once called never-never land? The most likely place in the world.

EPILOGUE

Six weeks later

THE SUN WAS already blazing in the eastern sky, and, even though it was early October, it looked like another hot one. Tacy paused on the threshold to the kitchen and took a deep breath, enjoying the scene unfolding before her. Timmy was at the table, slurping a cup of orange juice and chattering about his plans for the day. Her grandfather appeared to be reading the newspaper, but the twinkle in his eye suggested that his attention was on his great-grandson rather than the headlines.

"Tacy-girl." Her grandfather spotted her standing by the door. "Come and join us. I've got oatmeal on the stove and coffee in the percolator."

"Yeah, and Mom, you better eat fast. Remember we have to set up for the softball game this morning," Timmy chimed in.

She grabbed a bowl from the cupboard and helped herself to breakfast.

It was still hard to believe that six weeks had passed since the confrontation on the cliff. So many things had changed since then. She sipped her coffee and considered again how very different life was now. She and Timmy had moved in with her grandfather at the ranch. Timmy had started school, and as soon as she got the news that she had passed the bar, she applied for reciprocity in North Dakota and found legal work checking deeds and handling property disputes. It wasn't what she had envisioned when she had graduated law school. But little did she know how much better and richer a life God had planned for her. She still thought about her dad every day, but having her grandfather back in her life eased some of the pain.

Admittedly, she missed some elements of the city, the small luxuries of everyday life. A grocery store within walking distance. Parks. Sidewalks. And yet, when she had returned to Denver four weeks ago to pack up her old apartment, she'd realized that, although she had been happy there, it hadn't been home. A glance through her father's possessions proved it. She hadn't realized how much of his life in North Dakota he had held on to until she had dug into his closet and discovered all the keepsakes he had kept hidden away. A buffalo-shaped coffee mug. His old cowboy boots and hat. Pictures—of the ranch, of her as a little girl, of her grandfather. Nostalgia panged in her chest, but it was tinged with happiness and gratitude.

"Mom! Mom!" Timmy's voice cut through her musings. "You have to hurry. We only have a half hour before we're supposed to arrive."

She nodded her head as Timmy bounded away. Of course. The softball game. With the Hunts and all their ranch hands. And, of course, Seb. Her heart somersaulted. Even though they saw each other every day, she still felt a thrill every time their glances met or he held her hand. They both seemed to understand the blessing of this second chance.

She checked the time on the microwave. Eight forty. She really did have to hustle. The game was scheduled for nine, and her grandfather was a stickler about being on time.

Twenty minutes later, they arrived at the field, all decked out in custom T-shirts identifying them as Team Tolbert.

"You really don't mind?" she asked her grandfather. "Spending the day with the Hunts?"

"Of course not." His voice was craggy but sure. Since she and Timmy had moved in with him at the ranch, his life had changed in a big way too. After the shock of his wife's and trusted attorney's betrayal, he had stopped the sale of his property. He was even considering leasing a part of his land to Steven. "We buried the hatchet the day that you and Seb saved Timmy on Shepherd's Peak. In fact, have you had the chance to draw up the new water rights lease? I told Scott we'd get it taken care of asap."

Tacy hid a smile. Somehow, amidst all of the turmoil and change of the last few weeks, Scott Hunt and her grandfather had become friends. "I've got it drafted. I just need to double-check a couple of terms."

Her grandfather gave a nod and then hurried over to chalk the line between the bases. Tacy watched him for a moment and then turned her eyes toward the handsome, dark-haired man making his way toward her. Her heart thudded as Seb pulled her in for quick kiss.

"I like your shirt," he commented.

"Right back atcha." She laughed at the handwritten letters across the front of his shirt. "Hunt Squad."

Tolberts versus Hunts. The game started out slow, but excitement mounted in the sixth inning.

"Hit it out of the park," Timmy cheered as Tacy came up to bat. Although no one was officially keeping score, Timmy and her grandfather were maintaining a tally in their head. And currently, Team Tolbert was down by two with Len on second and the tying run at the plate.

Steven did an elaborate wind-up and pitched his trademark change-up, but she was ready. With a swing, she made contact and sent the ball sailing into the air.

And she was off, running with all her might. One of the Hunts' ranch hands must have stopped the liner in the infield because she could see Seb at first base preparing to make the play.

Maybe she could beat the throw. Ten more feet. Eight. She picked up her pace, her foot making contact with the base just seconds before Seb caught the ball.

"Out!" Scott Hunt bellowed from the outfield.

Out? She was clearly safe. She fixed Seb with a steely glare. "I was safe."

Seb shrugged. "My dad's the umpire, and he called 'out.'"

She turned around to catch the eye of her grandfather and Timmy. Surely they would agree that it had been an unfair call. But no. They smiled and waved. She turned back around.

What?

Her heart thudded and a slow flush crept up her neck.

Seb was down on one knee. He reached forward and took her hand. Her eyes filled with tears even before he began to speak.

"Tacy, I love you. More than I did ten years ago. More than I did yesterday. But this time I want to do things right. Will you do me the honor of marrying me in front of God, our friends and family?"

Tears rolled down her cheeks, but she didn't bother to wipe them away. "Yes," she said.

Seb pulled out a box out of his pocket and opened the lid. A familiar gold band nestled on a bed of velvet. It was the same ring he had given her ten years earlier.

"How did you…?" she sputtered.

"Your grandfather found it in your jewelry box when I asked for his blessing. Timmy's too. They both agreed that it's high time we became a family."

He slipped the ring on her finger. It still fit.

"Oh, and one more thing. Dad called you out because we thought our teams needed a little shake-up. No more Team Tolbert or Hunt Squad." He lifted his shirt. Then, everyone on the field did the same thing.

Underneath they all wore shirts with a new logo. Hunt + Tolbert = Family.

"What are you waiting for?" Seb asked, tossing a folded shirt her way. "Get back on base. We've got a game to finish. And a future to build here in Chimney Bluff."

* * * * *

If you enjoyed this book,
pick up these other exciting
stories from Love Inspired Suspense.

Tracking a Kidnapper
by Valerie Hansen

Hidden Witness
by Shirlee McCoy

Alaskan Showdown
by Sarah Varland

Accidental Target
by Theresa Hall

Under Suspicion
by Sommer Smith

Find more great reads at
www.LoveInspired.com

Dear Reader,

When I was in fifth grade, my teacher found a clever way to deal with cliques in the classroom. It was a little rhyme, and it went like this: "Secrets, secrets, are no fun. Secrets, secrets, hurt someone. NO SECRETS!"

In *Fatal Ranch Reunion*, Tacy's determination to keep Timmy's birth a secret hurt a lot of people. Of course, the deception wasn't her fault alone. And not all secrets carry such momentous consequences. But in this case, Tacy's duplicity denied Seb precious time with his son and further fragmented the trust between their families. Whatever the nature of our earthly secrets, one thing is certain. We can always trust the Lord. "For there is nothing covered, that shall not be revealed; neither hid, that shall not be known." Luke 12:2

It has been my great joy to share Tacy and Seb's story with you, I love hearing from my readers. You can contact me on Facebook at https://www.facebook.com/jaycee.bullard.1 or Instagram at https://www.instagram.com/jceebullard/?hl=en.

Jaycee Bullard

Get 4 FREE REWARDS!

We'll send you 2 FREE Books plus 2 FREE Mystery Gifts.

Love Inspired books feature uplifting stories where faith helps guide you through life's challenges and discover the promise of a new beginning.

FREE
Value Over
$20

THE WESTERN HEARTS COLLECTION!

COWBOYS. RANCHERS. RODEO REBELS.
Here are their charming love stories in one prized Collection:
51 emotional and heart-filled romances that capture the majesty
and rugged beauty of the American West!

YES! Please send me **The Western Hearts Collection** in Larger Print. This collection begins with 3 FREE books and 2 FREE gifts in the first shipment. Along with my 3 free books, I'll also get the next 4 books from The Western Hearts Collection, in LARGER PRINT, which I may either return and owe nothing, or keep for the low price of $5.45 U.S./$6.23 CDN each plus $2.99 U.S./$7.49 CDN for shipping and handling per shipment*. If I decide to continue, about once a month for 8 months I will get 6 or 7 more books but will only need to pay for 4. That means 2 or 3 books in every shipment will be FREE! If I decide to keep the entire collection, I'll have paid for only 32 books because 19 books are FREE! I understand that accepting the 3 free books and gifts places me under no obligation to buy anything. I can always return a shipment and cancel at any time. My free books and gifts are mine to keep no matter what I decide.

☐ 270 HCN 5354   ☐ 470 HCN 5354

Name (please print)

Address   Apt. #

City   State/Province   Zip/Postal Code

Mail to the **Reader Service:**
IN U.S.A.: P.O. Box 1341, Buffalo, N.Y. 14240-8531
IN CANADA: P.O. Box 603, Fort Erie, Ontario L2A 5X3